THE GHOST VARIATIONS

✦ THE ✦
GHOST VARIATIONS

ONE HUNDRED STORIES

Kevin Brockmeier

PANTHEON BOOKS, NEW YORK

All rights reserved. Published in the United States by Pantheon Books, a division of Penguin Random House LLC, New York, and distributed in Canada by Penguin Random House Canada Limited, Toronto.

Pantheon Books and colophon are registered trademarks of Penguin Random House LLC.

Library of Congress Cataloging-in-Publication Data
Name: Brockmeier, Kevin, author.
Title: The ghost variations : one hundred stories / Kevin Brockmeier.
Description: First edition. New York : Pantheon Books, 2021.
Identifiers: LCCN 2020001483 (print). LCCN 2020001484 (ebook).
ISBN 9781524748838 (hardcover). ISBN 9781524748845 (ebook).
Subjects: LCSH: Ghost stories, American.
Classification: LCC PS3602.R63 G56 2020 (print) |
LCC PS3602.R63 (ebook) | DDC 813/.6—dc23
LC record available at lccn.loc.gov/2020001483
LC ebook record available at lccn.loc.gov/2020001484

www.pantheonbooks.com

Jacket design and illustration by Kelly Blair

Printed in the United States of America

First Edition
2 4 6 8 9 7 5 3 1

It is not hard to imagine a ghost successfully. What is hard is successfully to imagine an object, any object, that does *not* look like a ghost.

—ELAINE SCARRY, *Dreaming by the Book*

Tell me what you see vanishing and I
Will tell you who you are

—W. S. MERWIN, "For Now"

Contents

GHOSTS AND TIME

GHOSTS AND SPECULATION

GHOSTS AND VISION

GHOSTS AND THE OTHER SENSES

GHOSTS AND BELIEF

GHOSTS AND LOVE AND FRIENDSHIP

GHOSTS AND FAMILY

GHOSTS AND WORDS AND NUMBERS

GHOSTS

✦ AND ✦

MEMORY

ONE

A NOTABLE SOCIAL EVENT

The ghost in the law firm's doorway never stops leaving. Every few seconds she glides across the threshold of the exit, steps suddenly to her left, raises the back of her right hand to her cheek, and starts over, her face bearing a sunken look of hard concentration. She does not *return* to the spot where she began exactly. She *recurs* there. Her irises are white with death, her skin silver, her hair a gray-green Spanish moss. A hundred and seven years ago, in this very hall, when the law firm's warren of desks and tables was a ballroom with red oak parquetry and a hammered tin ceiling, the young physician on whose attentions she had set her heart had spurned her for the linener's daughter, putting his lips to her plump pink knuckles and declaring his infatuation before the entire room. Back then the ghost was only a living girl of fifteen. Though she tried to leave furtively, at the doorway she stumbled into someone's man-servant, a tall oak post of a fellow who punctured the silence between waltzes with "I do beg your pardon, miss," and then, seeing the tears on her cheeks, "Are you not well?" The girl lifted her hand to her face in a spasm of embarrassment, then ran off into the square.

Now she repeats the same maneuver again and again, but with a million minor variations: raising or lowering her elbow;

rotating her ankle a quarter-inch to the right; pivoting her waist to move the bustle of her gown. She flees through the door, then flees through the door again. She brings her hand to her cheek, this time as if to fend off a blow, the next as if to swat at an insect, the next as if to test for a fever. She separates her fingers slightly. She adjusts the angle of her wrist. It is not for shame that she haunts these few square feet of the law office but for the inadequacy of the original gesture. At fifteen, she thinks, she failed to express the true complexity of her emotions, all her humiliation, resentment, forlornness, and heartache, each feeling in its exact proportions, and so, ever since she died, she has performed her flight from the ballroom with countless tiny reinflections. She is like a singer who cannot stop trying to perfect a particular syllable. When she was alive she spoke the moment—in truth she mumbled it—and now she is trying to sing it. Sometimes, in the long hours of a summer afternoon, when the paralegals at their desks are seeking a distraction, they watch the ghost emerging from her pleat in space and time and wonder if their lives will slip by like hers did, leaving them fastened so hopelessly, so desperately, to the past. As if a life could work any other way. As if that weren't precisely what a life must do.

TWO

THE GUIDANCE COUNSELOR

"This has never happened before." The guidance counselor brandished the printout like a lawyer presenting an annihilating piece of evidence, though in truth he was amused: playacting. "It seems that you're ideally suited to be, one, a conductor, or two, an actuary. So far, so good, presuming you like music and statistics. But then there's number three. Maybe they mean a *host*? Here, why don't you take a look." He offered the page to the girl, who sat unassumingly in one of his office's sprung vinyl armchairs. She was his fourteenth student of the day. Without a file to consult, he could not remember who she was, her GPA, how she had tested or which extracurriculars she boasted, but in almost forty years on the job, he had developed a knack for swift appraisals. So then: a grayish girl with wiry hair and jeans that bunched at the knees. Quiet and deferential. Not a troublemaker. Not even a nonconformist. To his best assessment a classic B student, which made her career aptitude results all the more ridiculous. She read the page, creased it smartly down the center, and, smiling almost invisibly, glanced at the wall clock. She said, "We still have twenty-five seconds. I don't see why we can't get an early start, though. Come with me." The girl led him into the lobby, where a tall bank of tempered glass windows showed the blue sky, a few tousled-looking pine trees, and the car dealership across the street. The guidance counselor was not sure why he had allowed himself to follow her. Letting his counselees believe they were in charge almost never ended well. He was usually smarter than this. He remembered what it was like to be their age, tantalized by dreams and visions—pianist! novelist! movie star!—all those sunlit futures you imagined for yourself before you took out a loan, enrolled in the nearest state college, and earned your ed. psych. degree. The guidance counselor had never married; had hardly even dated. It was better, easier, he had decided, not to disturb anyone with his love or his sadness. And, honestly, he found more fulfillment in the commotion of the high school, with all its teenage theatrics and uncertainties, than he did anywhere else. Take right now: the halls were bustling, turbulating, as though the bell had just rung, but an elemental silence presided over the scene. It was not the usual vortex of students and teachers, though, who engulfed him, but something else: a crowd of ghosts. In a single fixed moment, he watched the light shining through them, the sparks of dust that pierced them like comets, watched their strange underwater way of moving, and the stillness on their faces, the repletion. Ghosts, he thought: no question. When he tried to speak, he found that he could not use his voice. But the grayish girl with the wiry hair nodded as if she understood him anyway. She stroked his cheek. She took his hand. Her eyes were full of kindness.

THREE

A HATCHET, SEVERAL CANDLESTICKS, A PINCUSHION, AND A TOP HAT

The man keeps waking from dreams he has presumed, while sleeping, to be real, then apprehending, through some commonplace object pregnant with dream-meaning, that they must have happened after all. Every morning the same dumb story. Just now, for instance, he sat up suddenly in his bed, centuries and continents away from the beautiful green-eyed princess whose devotion he won by vanquishing a dragon, and then discovered, to his surprise, that he was clutching her locket and chain. He draped it from his bedpost. It nestled there against the locket of the prairie schoolteacher who mistook him for her long-lost son, and the locket of the stage actress who was also, to the rapture of her fans, a swarm of yellowjackets, and the locket of the Russian countess who posed watertight riddles to her suitors and then had them killed, and a dozen others like it, all of them transported out of dreams he had perceived as actual until he awoke, when he deduced that he had merely been sleeping, until he noticed the object in his hand and he realized that he hadn't. Most of the items he has woken with are similarly small and trinkety: a key, a coin, a pencil. But he has also found himself carrying full-length mirrors, fur coats, and soup tureens, as well as saddles, croquet mallets, feather dusters, a Bunsen burner, a mortadella sausage, wigs, a toy train set, a Van de Graaff generator, a papermaking press, and even, once, a sofa. From every corner he is confronted with memories of the worlds he has visited. He cannot see the abacus on his nightstand without recalling the ghost of that lady with the broken fingers, proud and despondent, who both haunted and was in love with him. The stethoscope on his dresser reminds him of that city where he slipped into a whirlpool of vaned glass marbles. This little apartment, with its inundation of keepsakes—he half-expects to waken from it, too, one day, clutching a toothbrush in his hand, or a wallet. What a tragedy it would be, he thinks, what a joke, if the best, worst, strangest, and most extravagant hours of his life were spent escaping it. He throws back his covers and lifts himself out of bed. The lockets on his bedpost jingle like a puppy. More and more it seems to him that all the certainty in his life, if not the pleasure, is concentrated in the approximately eight seconds of confusion, bereavement, relief, or exultation he experiences each morning when he is convinced his dreams have abandoned him. In truth those eight seconds are the only time, when he *is* awake, that he does not doubt it.

FOUR

MILO KRAIN

"Sign the petition?" The old man standing outside the bakery does not ask the question so much as gruffs it, summoning the words up from someplace deep in his body. The other man, younger and fitter, stopping off for a loaf of ciabatta and a bottle of red on his way home from the office, hunches into his suit and attempts to parry past him, but again the first man says, "Sign the petition? Sign the petition to addle Milo Krain?" And at this the younger man pauses. For two reasons the question strikes him as peculiar: first that exotic verb, so casually deployed, as if "addling" someone were the most ordinary of human activities; but second, and chiefly, because he is Milo Krain. He steels himself, then makes up his mind, swiveling back around to face the man with the petition. "Pardon me," he inquires, "did I hear you say something about Milo Krain?" Immediately the older man's carriage changes. He smiles deferentially and extends a brown Masonite clipboard. "Would you like to sign our petition, sir? I assure you it's for a worthy cause." The dispirited note in his voice has been replaced by a salesmanlike zing. When Milo asks, "And what cause might that be?" the man taps his clipboard for emphasis. "Well, sir, we'd like to ensure that the initiative to addle Milo Krain moves forward as planned. As you know, the population of ghosts, specters, and demons approved this measure overwhelmingly, but there's been a rumble among some of the council members to dismiss Mr. Krain with only a few seconds of mild disorientation. Now, I ask you, is that fair?" "But," Milo begins, "I'm—" and though he hesitates, he must unintentionally say the name out loud, because the man with the clipboard summons a second man with a clipboard and tells him, "You'll never believe it, but this fellow claims *he's* Milo Krain." The two of them look him up and down. Their skin, he notices, on this, the most sunstruck day of the whole blue winter, glistens—or no: effervesces. It is as if they are caught inside a rain that affects only them, not the pebbled concrete of the sidewalk, not the cars idling at the curb, not the shoppers parading in and out of the bakery and sending gusts of yeasty air through the doors. After some *Is-that-so?*-ing and *It-hardly-seems-likely*-ing, the two men appear to come to a decision. One of them says to Milo Krain, "I'm afraid you're mistaken," and the other adds, "Yes, that's right. You're not Milo Krain. You're not Milo Krain at all." And suddenly they are gone, just two clipboards that fall to the ground without clattering, because they don't in fact exist, and he is a man without a name, standing alone in a heathered wool suit, most thoroughly addled.

FIVE

AMNESIA

The luminous strangers offer their hands to her. With kindness and pity they say, "Do not be frightened," and she is not frightened. They say, "You will not remember us," and she does not remember them. "You've returned," they assuage her. "That's the important thing."

Their faces are like sunlight on water, a thousand tumbling jacks of white and silver. They gather around her so closely, and in such shifting numbers, that she worries—or rather she ought to worry; she designates worry as a possibility—that they will crush her, but their bodies ride the air so weightlessly, and she feels so weightless among them, that she trusts they will not do so. By what turn she might have arrived here, what alleyway or open door, she cannot recollect. It occurs to her that she is not wearing the shoes she put on this morning. Nor, it would seem, the dress or the jacket. She took the subway to work. That she is sure of. The motor was out at the terminal, and she had to climb the escalator as though it were an ordinary staircase, but the cleated steps with their strange distribution of measurements, a little too deep and a little too tall, along with the curving metal fins of the risers, made her feel as if she was scaling the teeth of some enormous saw. For a moment she thought the tunnel's exit had gone topsy-turvy and she was climbing down instead of up. A dizziness at the temples, a gust of warm air, and suddenly, all around her, the luminous strangers. They swaddle her now on every side, including, improbably, above and below. The sky, the ground, are bright with their faces: ablaze. Their features are so changeable that if they do not fuse together, she thinks, they will surely burn apart. But they do not fuse together. They do not burn apart. Instead they ripple.

The luminous strangers say, "We are your brothers and sisters." And they are exactly that: her brothers and sisters. They say, "Soon you will feel at home here again." And she does feel at home there—even, she is willing to believe, again. They say, "One day, presently, you will understand." And one day, presently, she does. She was alive for a while, and before that she was not, and now she is not all over again. But the nonbeing from which she emerged and the post-being into which she has graduated are not quite the same. Nor is she the same privileged spirit she used to be, lulled by the comforts of home, so sure that, unlike the others, she would awaken one day and remember where she had come from.

A LONG CHAIN OF YESTERDAYS

Not for the first time, or even the hundredth, the bank president stands at his office window at 6:03 on the evening of Tuesday, March 3, 1987. Two birds square off on the other side of the glass, bickering over what looks like a raisin. The sky is as pink as cupcake frosting. Far below him a delivery truck triggers its horn, an agitated sound that the distance transforms into an adorable beep. The scene is so calming, so toylike, that originally, for one bare minute, smack in the middle of his life, it suffused the bank president with a sense of inexplicable peace, a bone-deep certainty that everything would be all right. But after the eighth repetition, or the nineteenth, he noticed that at this time of day, on this date, the horn *always* beeps adorably, the birds *always* nip at the raisin, the sky is *always* a cupcake pink. Thus the bank president feels overcome, despite the beauty and charm of it all, by the tedium, the invariability. He knows that his ennui is not March 3, 1987, at 6:03's fault—not specifically. Every other moment is just as static. Take 11:24 on the morning of Friday, July 26, 1940. It is his older sister's eighth birthday. He is drinking lemonade in the backyard. His elbows are reddening against the picnic table, and a coiled paper party horn is crimping to the left as he blows through it. Or 4:36 a.m. on Wednesday, December 6, 1972. He is watching the color bars on a hotel TV and crunching the ice from a gin and tonic. Idly he plucks at the hangnail on his thumb, then strips it loose with his front teeth. The cold of the ice on his lips deadens the sting. Or three in the afternoon on Thursday, August 10, 2006. He is trekking through the rough after a golf ball when his heart makes a fist around itself. Then he is lying on his back beneath a catalpa tree with a V-shaped trunk. The leaves vary their patterns of lighter and darker green as the wind bats them around in the sunlight. He remembers his pleasure upon discovering, after his heart stopped, that as a ghost he could revisit any moment of his life, as many times as he wanted to. Any minute, though, no matter how extraordinary, will harden into its form if it happens the same way often enough, he soon discovered. Eventually, the bank president worries, he will forget that he is a ghost. That this endless series of repetitions is not his life. Will forget how it felt when things could still happen for the first time. For now, though, he stands once more at his office window. It is 6:03 on the evening of Tuesday, March 3, 1987. Despite the pinkness of the sky, the streetlights have already been kindled, long rows of dots that, for reasons he does not understand, seem to grow brighter the farther away they are.

GHOSTS

✦ AND ✦

FORTUNE

SEVEN

THE HITCHHIKER

The hitchhiker who asks her if she is going to Toledo is, of course, the Grim Reaper. He is not the first such hitchhiker she has encountered. Nor will he be the last. His appearance at the side of the road is a sign and a demonstration that she has died but does not yet know it. At least once a day, and usually more often, a man with thinning hair and a sun-blasted face, or baggy clothes and large O-shaped nostrils, or a wiry frame and eyes the color of creek moss, will walk up to her car while she is paused in traffic, and in a voice that reminds her of sand cascading over sand, soft and rustling but also bonelike, arthritic, he will ask her about Toledo. One memorable Tuesday she met twelve of them—a record.

She died, she is reasonably sure, some seventeen years ago. She was visiting a state park in Colorado, admiring the panorama from a cliffside observation deck, when all at once she landed, dazed, in the ankles of a fir tree. She tested her limbs and stood up. She was fine, she judged. Her head was clear and her bones were miraculously unbroken, though she could already feel a bruise rounding out on her hip.

But that afternoon a hitchhiker at the park's entrance asked what so many thousands have asked her since: "Are you going to Toledo?" A few hitchhikers later and she suspected she was dead. Two or three more and she was certain of it. She was not an idiot. But as long as she feigns ignorance, she has determined, the hitchhikers will not collect, condemn, transform, exalt, or annihilate her. She can remain safely among the living, free to dine out or watch TV, garden or surf the web, in the light of this world rather than the murk of the next. To the hitchhikers' question, therefore, she always answers no, she is not going to Toledo. If, that is, she answers at all. Sometimes, when she is tired or hurried, she finds it easier just to tap her ear as though hard of hearing. At first her simplemindedness seemed to aggravate the hitchhikers. By what appalling failure of deduction could this woman continue to believe she was alive? It made no sense, she could see them marveling. Experimentally, for a year or two, they began approaching her in supermarkets, fitness centers, movie theaters, yoga studios— places where she could not, by any conceivable logic, and no matter how pointedly they asked, have been going to Toledo. But eventually they returned to the medians and street corners that were their natural milieu, waiting for her to realize that she had taken a fall and not survived.

These days, it seems to her, they have secretly given up. Oh, they continue to ask her about Toledo, but by habit and without expectation. After all, she can pretend to misapprehend the truth of her situation indefinitely. It is not difficult. She is convinced that her intransigence has revealed a loophole in the cosmic order. All she has to do, she reasons, is maintain the ruse each time she is questioned, no matter how often, and she will survive not only to a lustrous old age but also, and as it must be, forever.

EIGHT

WISHES

By now everyone understood the importance of articulating your wishes with the utmost specificity. This was why the woman with the magic lamp had not spoken aloud—or even written anything down—in three months and nine days, ever since the genie emerged in his perfume of rosemary and lit matches. One minuscule error of phrasing, she knew, and she would end up doomed, suffocating beneath an Everest of gold coins, or bound for life to a man whose love for her rendered him insipid, or ruling as queen over some muddy wasteland. No, it was better if she took her time, hiding herself away in the quiet little grammar laboratory of her mind. One day, when her wishes were unassailable, she would break her silence, but until then she would measure her words carefully, adding and removing parentheticals and fastidiously retailoring her syntax until every piece of every wish fit faultlessly together. What did it matter if she drained her savings along the way, or lost her friends, or weakened her health? After all, if she wished well enough, she could regain them in an instant.

The genie was sympathetic to her predicament. Over his many centuries of transforming wishes into curses, their inexactitudes and ambiguities had become all too conspicuous to him. Sometimes he imagined what it would be like to take a curry and brush to the things, grooming each and every wish until what people desired and what they asked for were actually identical. He had his role to play, though, and he was obligated to play it. The sequence of events hardly ever varied: someone would free him from his lamp and invoke the ritual words: first an "I" and then a "wish." Each time, with the pronunciation of that second syllable, a great roar of hope and affection would rise up inside him. Maybe, he would say to himself. Maybe this will be the one. The one who finally outwits me. The one who gets it right. Then, in an instant, the roar would come to a stop, overthrown by the hush of yet another person making yet another mistake, the awful empty death sound of good luck going bad. They were all the same, human beings, or at least the ones who summoned him from his vessel were. They wanted so much and brought such terrible misfortune on themselves.

The woman sat with her lips pressed tight in concentration, paging through her dictionary and her thesaurus. The genie stared down at her from atop the roiling cloud of his lower body. Three months or three days, three years or three seconds: time made no difference to him. Soon enough, he knew, she would squander her wishes and return him to his lamp, that verdigrised bronze prison where he was haunted by a thousand ghosts, all those clumsy wishers who blamed him for escorting their lives into disaster.

NINE

HOW TO PLAY

One: Select a Ghost Token. *Two:* Draw a coin from the Specter Stack to determine which room you will haunt. *Three:* Find the body-shaped pegs that match your Ghost in color. These are your Humans. Each of them is marked with two numbers, the first measuring their skepticism, the second their bravery. Hidden on the underside of each Human is a third number: their value in Ghost Points. Distribute your Humans across the board however you wish—but think strategically! *Four:* Take turns moving your Ghosts through the house by rolling the Spirit Dice. You may wander along the halls in any direction you choose, but you cannot double back until you reach one of the arrows on the board. *Five:* Each time you enter a room, draw a card from the Spook Stack. You may use these cards to switch squares with another Ghost, to pass through the walls of a room rather than the door, or to exorcise an opponent's Ghost from the Human of your choice—any one of thirty-six exciting possibilities! *Six:* If you land on a square with a Human who does not belong to you, you must attempt to possess him. Roll the Spirit Dice. If the number you throw is lower than the Human's skepticism, he fails to notice you and your turn is at an end. Otherwise, you should roll the dice again. If your second throw produces a number lower than the Human's bravery, you hide from him; equal to, you terrify him, and may send him fleeing to the square of your choice; higher than, you possess him, and may add his Ghost Points to your tally. *Seven:* If you land on a square occupied by another Ghost, you must attempt to expel it. Roll the Spirit Dice, and add the resulting number to your Ghost Points. If this sum is lower than your opponent's Ghost Points, the attempt has failed and your turn is over; higher than, and you should roll the dice to see how many of your opponent's Ghost Points you may absorb; equal to, and you may banish the Ghost you have attacked from the board entirely. *Eight:* The first Player either to haunt the entire House or possess every Human wins! Congratulations! *Nine:* The winner's Ghost may travel beyond the confines of the game. *Ten:* Select one of your fellow Players to haunt and follow him home. *Eleven:* Cause his electricity to flicker. Disrupt his sleep. Lower the temperature around his left hand by twenty degrees. Make his phone ring, exactly once, every night at precisely 2:15. Rot any food he brings to his mouth. Repel anyone who might otherwise have loved him. Magnify his sorrows. Vitiate his joy. *Twelve:* A month later, when the next game night—Yahtzee—rolls around, listen as the Players wonder what has happened to your opponent, has anyone heard from him lately, it's like he just up and vanished, and by the way, they will whisper when you leave the room, has anyone noticed how you've been lifting your glass to your lips without actually taking a sip, and how you laugh at every joke maybe, but artificially, and a beat too late? You seem so wan, they agree, so distant, as if you are somewhere else altogether.

TEN

THE SCALES OF FORTUNE

Here in the sidewalk café sits a man whose fortunes are in perfect balance. In him the good and the bad of life, the yin and the yang, equal each other exactly—and not just suppositionally, in a sooner-or-later sort of way, but immediately and down to the smallest grain. Right now, for instance, he is eating a sandwich so slippery with mayonnaise that three-quarters of the lettuce glissaded into his mouth on the very first bite: *bad*. The tomato, on the other hand, is uncommonly fresh and hearty, with the kind of delectably tart sweetness that must have belonged to the very first tomato—the tomato, he thinks, that gave tomatoes their name: *good*. Or a more material example: Last week, the man received a letter containing the news that he had been awarded a prestigious fellowship, complete with a two-year monthly cash stipend. He had just reached the "congratulations again" portion of the letter when a call came from his bank informing him that someone had drained his checking account. His life has been abundant with such episodes. More than abundant, glutted. He met his teenage girlfriend when she stopped to help him after he was clipped by a car walking home from school. Last spring he woke from root canal surgery to find that he had won a hard-fought election to his condo board. The day his grandfather died, his dog gave birth to four puppies. He was in first grade at the time, and had not even lost his baby teeth, but already he understood how the formula worked. The world was showing him his grandfather's worth in puppies—apparently, four. So you see, the interdependency of adversity and well-being is not a matter of philosophy for the man, much less religious belief, but a matter of direct and ongoing experience. He has never faced a moment when his luck was not keeping measure with itself, the good counterchecking the bad and vice versa. As a result he views his life not as a series of highs and lows but as a single continuous high-low, sometimes more expansive and sometimes less, but always averaging out at precisely the same level. He welcomes each difficulty with a leap of nervous excitement. With each stroke of luck he feels a twinge of anticipatory fear. He lives in dread of landing his dream job, falling in love, winning the lottery. Though he does not know it, the perfect balance of his fortunes necessitates the existence of another man, or rather two—one whose life has been only blessings, and another, complementary, whose life has been only catastrophe. The perfect imbalance of their fortunes balances out the perfect balance of the man's own. On one side of the planet, here in the sidewalk café, he sits finishing his sandwich, carelessly dabbing the sauce from his lips, while on the other, in all their excess, live those two contrary men, the first strong and wealthy, radiant with sensual pleasures, and the other unloved, overintelligent, swollen with pathogens, haunted by ghosts.

ELEVEN

A MOMENT, HOWEVER SMALL

A ghost with a poor sense of direction, distinguished among the company of ghosts for her amiability and her absentmindedness, took a wrong turn inside the house she was haunting, weaving left between the broom closet and the pretersensual ether, and found herself hundreds of miles away, on a busy street corner, where a light snow was dusting the air. Bewildered by the bustle and noise, she attempted to double back and return to the quiet rooms she considered home, but it was too late, for in the pandemonium of the crowd, she had forgotten the way. Such moments of disorientation were relatively familiar to her—if not exactly commonplace, then not exactly rare either—but always before, when her course led her astray, she would find herself within sight of another ghost, some kind soul who might point her to the door she was overlooking or the lane she had missed. Here among the living, barrowing themselves around inside their big heavy bodies, asking for help was not so easy. She waited for someone to notice her. When no one did, she selected an old woman with an alarmed-looking dog cinched into her purse. "Excuse me," the ghost with a poor sense of direction began, "I—" but though the dog barked and barked, the woman hobbled past her without so much as a glance. Next she tried a man in a business suit popping a breath mint into his mouth, then a skinny teenager with the rigid smile of someone trying to enthuse the chill from his body, and then a disheveled woman wearing a blue surgical mask. "You look like just the person to—" the ghost said, and, "I wonder if you might—" but they all ignored her, hurrying over the curb to wade into the torrent of cars. Not ten feet away, observing her efforts with a strange feeling of sleepy wonder, as if gazing into a fire, was a hot dog vendor. He had witnessed her appearance a few minutes earlier. Instantly he had known, from the way her pieces sifted together, that she was a ghost, though he had never seen a ghost before, nor indeed believed in them. Nervously he called her over to his cart. As soon as he understood her dilemma, he pointed out the orange utility numbers that were painted on the sidewalk. "You see that plus sign? You came out of the air a few feet above it, and maybe an inch or so to the left. I was watching." The ghost thanked him with her usual aura of distracted kindness. Then, just like that, she was gone. The man stood watching the spot where she had been. Not long ago he had turned sixty, an age when people hunger for a moment, however small, that will justify the years they have spent and those that still remain to them. In his bones he felt that his had just happened, on an ordinary street corner, in a snow so faint that it vanished before it touched the pavement.

TWELVE

A GATHERING

It was never the houses the ghosts were haunting. All along it was the people. And so, as the people succumbed to the virus, first in flecks and dots and then by the millions, the ghosts abandoned the houses, gathering instead around the sturdy, the solitary, the lucky, the survivors. The world of the dead lay skin to skin with the world of the living. From that nearby kingdom, so still and silent, the ghosts watched the epidemic spread. To them, it seemed like a lake rain, the kind that begins with a few silver pinpricks on the water, then boils up hard, everywhere and all at once, before ending with a flutter of breezeblown drops. Suddenly, in the wake of the storm, the world was lit with sunshine again. The only man alive to see it, though, was a wealthy recluse and neurotic, so beset by the embarrassments of society that he had withdrawn from it entirely. For him every conversation, every transaction, down to the briefest and most businesslike, had become yet another occasion for injury. Those countless social encounters, with their countless tiny cuts—cuts inflicted, cuts received, and the one just as painful to remember as the other. Those smiles preceded by telltale pauses. Those favors both sexual and financial. Those *what-do-you-think*s and *let-me-borrow-you-for-a-second*s. It had all been too much for him, too freighted with need and misunderstanding, and so years ago, with part of his fortune, he had purchased a small Tahitian island, the most isolated and self-sustaining he could find, free by an accident of geography from the handshakes, sneezes, hugs, and kisses that had spread the virus, and by a quirk of the breezes from the mosquitoes that had incubated it. From his bungalow amid the ferns and coconut palms he let the days and nights go by. He could pass entire months without seeing another human being, and often did. Instead he lay in his hammock, swaying lackadaisically. There were no more jets drawing chalk lines in the sky, no more boats bobbing distantly in the water, and surely, if the man had been paying the right sort of attention, he would have noticed that something was wrong. How could he have guessed, though, that as the numbers of the dead had increased, the space they occupied had contracted? By the time the virus had finished its work, they had settled around him as thick as butter. Against his body, no more than a cell's distance away, pressed something intangible, inquisitive, endlessly alert. It jockeyed slowly for position. It throbbed against the barriers of his life. A life so much emptier than it used to be, and so much less alone.

THIRTEEN

MIRA AMSLER

"That's *you!*" says the man seated next to her. "Congratulations!" and before she quite knows what is happening, the woman with the sheen of moisturizer on her face has been ushered onto the stage. The flash of the cameras creates a blue-and-green nimbus in her eyes. By the time her sight has cleared, someone has handed her a trophy topped with an upside-down silver teardrop, its two fat arms meeting at the center of its belly. Engraved on the plate are the words "Best Newcomer," and beneath them her name: Mira Amsler. All at once, high in her field of vision, she sees a punch flying at her face. She flinches. But it is only the black grill of the microphone, jutting at her emphatically like the beak of some predatory bird. Flustered, she says, "This is very unexpected. I didn't prepare a speech. I have to confess, in fact, that I don't quite understand where I am. As you see, I'm wearing my pajamas right now. Also, my hair is cinched back in a scrunchie. But thank you. Thank you very much. I appreciate it." Though she intends the remarks sincerely, they must sound like self-effacing humor, for a gust of warming laughter accompanies her as she leaves the stage. A voice declares, "We'll be back after this short break with more of the Forty-first Annual Spirits' Choice Awards." Mira wonders out loud at the announcement: What the *what* now? The man who congratulated her says, "This? It's the big night." "*What* big night?" Mira asks. "You know. *The* night. For honoring the most noteworthy recent achievements among the dead and the dying." "But I'm *not* dead," Mira interrupts, and the man says, "Oh, you dear thing you. You didn't let me finish: among the dead, the dying, or the *soon to have died*. The awards cover the entire calendar year. It looks as if you're scheduled to die on—" He pages through his program. "July the seventh." Mira's mind is abuzz with questions. The ceremony resumes, though, before she can decide which of them to ask. No sooner does the presenter open his envelope than once again she hears her name, this time for "Best Featured Performer in a Cataclysm or Disaster." From all the whoops, whistles, and back pats she receives, she gathers that she was the runaway favorite. At the microphone she says, "Is this about my vacation? What's going to happen? Should I cancel my tickets?" A few minutes later her name is called a third time, for "Funniest Mortal Blooper." The applause rushes over her like a driving rain. "And boy," chuckles the emcee, "is this one a doozy. Let's watch the footage again, shall we?" The lights dim and the clip begins to roll. Mira is already halfway up the stairs, but her legs won't take her any farther. She halts there, a few steps from the apron of the stage, awaiting the ravages of her next award.

GHOSTS

✦ AND ✦

NATURE

FOURTEEN

ELEPHANTS

A pachydermologist was studying the vocalizations of African elephants. One day, listening to his latest field recordings, he looked up to find that just a few meters beyond the camp's cluster of canvas tents, where the yellow dirt was stitched to the yellow grass, the entire herd had gathered as if for a performance. He pressed the pause button on his stereo. All at once the elephants bustled with activity, tilting their heads, shouldering each other, and pendulating their trunks and tails. He pressed play and immediately they froze again, training their ears this way and that. How curious, the pachydermologist thought. Over the next hour he repeated the experiment a dozen times, always to the same result. Pause and then play. Pause and then play. Whenever the stereo was operating, the herd silenced itself. As soon as it ceased, they broke their repose. Moreover, he realized, their attention gravitated to a different elephant, or set of elephants, after each playback, depending on which set of rumbles, snorts, and trumpets had emerged from the speakers. How, they seemed to be asking each other, did you *do* that? Here you are, yet I heard you over there. How can you be calling from two places at once? Even to a bone-born behaviorist such as he, the conclusion was obvious: the members of the herd were capable not only of identifying individual voices—this much was already established science—but of identifying them *from recordings*. The question then became, were they able to distinguish the original voices, the live voices, from the reproductions? Several weeks of additional observation brought the pachydermologist no closer to an answer. Out of curiosity he devised a test. From his catalogue he retrieved an old recording: the bonding calls of a matriarch who had been killed for her ivory some six months earlier. He concealed the speakers in an area of brush and thorn, then retreated to a safe distance and activated the remote control. The elephants roared excitedly, trampling across the savanna. Every so often they halted to lift their trunks and reposition their ears, their enormous bodies moving as one as they attempted to sound out the matriarch's hiding place. Even after the calls stopped, the herd continued to search for her. For days her oldest daughter would not eat or drink. She stood on the dry bank of the creek, showering herself woefully with dust. Years later, when asked at a lecture to name his biggest professional regret, the pachydermologist remained too ashamed by this incident to recount it. For the elephants, though, it became the founding tale in a new age of ghost stories. Listen, my children, to a chronicle of wonder and sorrow. The-ghost-who-hid-in-high-grass. The-ghost-who-hissed-like-seven-snakes. The-ghost-who-came-back-and-left-again.

FIFTEEN

THE WHITE MARE

A pet medium, famed for her ability to communicate with dead and missing animals, heard the bells on her front door jingle. A man ducked into the parlor. He was dark and brawny, very somber, and, to her psychic antennae, neither a cat person nor a dog person. Right away this marked him as unusual. Ninety-nine percent of her clients could be picked out immediately as tremulous or distraught pet owners, who sought her out specifically to make contact with the ghost of a dear lost dog or cat. More unusual still was the hat he wore: a gold circlet, shaped to a dozen points, and weighty enough to leave a red dent on his forehead. In earlier centuries, or on a more regal cranium, one would have called it a crown, yet he wore it, she observed, without embarrassment, and without posturing. She had not yet introduced herself when he declared that he wished to know the whereabouts of a particular horse. "You are worried," said the pet medium. "That I can see," and asked him for a description of the animal. Curtly he answered, "White," as if more than one horse of the color were unimaginable. "Male?" she asked. "Female?" "A mare." The creature, the man continued, was essential to his duties. To his shame, however, he had released her bridle and she had bolted. Worse yet, she was carrying his bow and quiver in her straps. "Without her my work will be impossible," he said, "and time is distressingly short."

The pet medium put some iron in her spine. She pressed her hands to the table. Of course she would try her best, she announced, but the voices were fickle, the spirits could be diffident, and she was older than she used to be, her powers not so formidable. All of this was patter—a mere show—like the heavy eyeliner she wore, the iridescent scarf. Never once had she failed to find an animal she sought. In fact, with barely a psychic nudge, the location of the man's horse rang out in her mind like a gong. She had no need to consult her maps. He would recover his animal at the city park, she told him, grazing on the ryegrass near the smaller of the two fountains, though at this time of day, she added, with the Seventh down to one lane for repaving, the trains would be quicker than a taxi. The man fished a few coins from a pouch and said, "I thank you." Watching him rise from his chair, the pet medium was graced with a thought—that of the many eccentrics who had passed through her door, and the many fools she had counseled, he was the most eccentric, and the least foolish. The room seemed to flatten as he left it. For the next fifteen minutes or so her candles, crystals, and dreamcatchers looked like so many silly gewgaws. Then she heard the hooves tattooing the street, and went to the door, and saw the dark man with his crown and his bow, astride his white horse, spreading pestilence with the drop of each arrow.

SIXTEEN

MANY ADDITIONAL ANIMALS

The pill that could reveal the two animals of which a person was the fusion was an immediate sensation. It worked swiftly, precisely, and painlessly. Just swallow a green-and-yellow capsule with Y77 printed on the casing, wait three to four minutes, and you would understand with a decisiveness that foreclosed all questioning that you were a combination of a muskrat and a bison, or a goose and a spider, not only apparently but to the bottom of your character. The knowledge washed through you with the quality of a proclamation, dissolving all at once and categorically into your bloodstream. A woman who discovered herself to be a bobcat and a kite would think yes, of course, here it was—her feline gracefulness, her raptorial shrewdness, the key to her, the why. A man who was an armadillo and a seahorse would realize that the pill explained his oddity, his defendedness, his susceptibility to colds and illnesses, even his secret wish to carry a clutch of children in his belly. The evidence and the verdict were one and the same. It was all so obvious, so logical. People hosted pill parties where the guests tried to speculate, based on intuition and acquaintance, which two animals the capsule would reveal in one another. "She's a porpoise and a greyhound." "No, she's half deer and half gazelle." "Something wily and dangerous, I'd say, like a hornet and maybe a wolf"—and everyone but the woman in question would be delighted when, despite all their predictions, she was discovered to be a snail and a pelican. Animals, too, were given the pill, often in labs or clinics, where it was determined that, just like people, each of them was a synthesis of two disparate animals. Frequently one of those inner animals turned out to be a human being—though never among the other primates, oddly enough, and a cat was always a cat and a cat. For several years it was common for men and women who shared a particularly desirable inner species to have children with the idea of passing that animal along to the next generation. The normal genetic procedures, however, seemed not to apply. Even two parents who were both, at their core, a horse and a ram might produce one child who was a porcupine and an ant and another who was a rhinoceros and a bear. The science of it was inexplicable. The religion of it, on the other hand, thrived. A belief took hold even among practicing evangelicals that when your life was over you became not a singular human soul but the souls of that pair of animals of whom or by which you had been constituted. Some people imagined such an eternity to be a comfort; others a damnation. The difference lay chiefly in whether they felt themselves to be a hybrid or a chimera—something, in other words, that ought all along to have existed, or something that ought all along not to.

SEVENTEEN

BEES

They are not, strictly speaking, bees. They are bee-*shaped:* velvety round blurs with a pin at one end. They are bee-*sized:* as big as a thumb from the tip to the knuckle. And they *move* like bees, bobbing, darting, looping, and swerving in a dizzy, vacillating dance. But though it is tempting to think of them as bees, they are not bees. They have no wings, for instance; no venom. They fly silently, without buzzing. And while they toil as bees do, working over what one might call their fields, it is neither pollen they gather nor nectar. One additional difference, which should not be overlooked: though they exert themselves like bees, and though they luxuriate like bees, they are not, like bees, alive. They make their home on the periphery between life and death, plying their way along the emptiness of the border—that almost inconceivably thin line where bodies become something other than bodies and time commingles with eternity. There the bees assemble their hives, great lobes of interjoining cells that shake and pulse with their activity. In chains and waves the bees depart from the hives and return. The paths they trace seem partially intentional and partially haphazard, so that it is impossible to tell when they are maintaining their course and when they are altering it, only that, however they select their coordinates, they fix themselves over the recently dead the way real bees do over flowers. They operate, that is to say, with instinct if not with purpose. Unfailingly, as soon as someone begins to flicker through their little boundary world, one of the bees will upend itself and prick at him. That they are harvesting something is plain. Energy. Ghosts. The shadow structures of matter. They carry that something with them, whatever it might be, as they dip from person to person. Then they retreat, fat with it, to their hives. Really that is all there is to this place: the bees, the hives, and a great host of forms passing rapidly out of their humanity. All that remains to be said is this: that the threshold the bees navigate is penetrable from either side, which is to say that people cross over it not only as they die, traveling out of history and into infinity, but also as they are born, traveling out of infinity and into history. The bees, it would seem, cannot distinguish between the first set of forms and the second. If indeed these people are something like flowers, and if the substance the bees collect is something like pollen, one can only wonder who is pollinating whom, and whether it is the living who fertilize the dead or the dead who fertilize the living.

EIGHTEEN

A BLIGHT ON THE LANDSCAPE

It occurred to him that the tens of millions of trees discoloring the landscape were destined to outlive him, and so insulted was he by the realization that he vowed to exterminate as many as he could. By eighteen he had logged the last remaining oak from his family's farm, by thirty-five he had become the most successful commercial real estate developer in the South, and by sixty-four, when he died, he had razed whole cities' worth of timber, replacing the hickories, willows, pines, and cottonwoods with shopping centers, parking lots, and office complexes where the only surviving vegetation stood in queerly shaped crooks and triangles, as sparse as the hair under his arms. A more productive life he could not have imagined. When he woke as a ghost, surrounded by the ghosts of those same tens of millions of trees, his indignation was boundless. The woods seemed neverending, a flickering maze of trunks beneath a riot of dreamlike foliage. Something like a breeze winnowed its way through their branches. Something like the sun glowed behind their leaves. Surely, he thought, this was Hell. A night passed and a day. The man struck out in search of a clearing. But no matter where he went, he found more trees plugging the air. It was many weeks later, and only by chance, that he figured out how to kill them. A simple axe blow of the hand, delivered with just the right focused malevolence, and down they would crash, plunging to the earth in a cataract of bark and twigs. Maybe *not* Hell, he thought. Maybe Heaven. Tree by tree he worked his way through the forest, until one day, as it was falling, a large maple swung about-face and flattened him. Apparently ghosts could die, because when he woke again he was in a new place—not just a ghost but the ghost of a ghost. The soil was richer here, the air warmer, and all around him were more goddamned trees, assaulting his eyes with their faded browns and greens. These were harder to kill than the others had been, their trunks thicker and frogged with knots. The next time he died, the trees were as small and slender as dandelions, and he was able to mow them down by the thousands. The time after that they were mostly water, and spilled from their outlines with the easiest of pokes. And the time after *that* they gave him a rash that slowly proved fatal. Finally one day, the ghost of a ghost of a ghost of a ghost, he woke to find that his feet were rooted to the soil. Struggle though he might, he could not free them. Worse were the trees themselves, great mobs of bark and sap that went rushing past him like pedestrians at a street fair. They kept bruising him with their limbs, the horrifying beasts. Cones and nuts bombed down at him from their canopies. Their heavy steps expelled the rank smell of vegetation, yet they seemed unaware of him. If he stayed perfectly still, he thought, perfectly still and silent, if he did not wince or cry out, there was the slimmest of chances that they would not notice him. Knock on wood.

NINETEEN

AN OSSUARY OF TREES

The night it occurred to him he was living inside a corpse—or, to be more precise, inside the bones of a hundred corpses: the trees that constituted the timbers of his house—was the same night he stopped sleeping. His daylight troubles were the same as everyone else's: the bills that needed paying; the work that needed doing; the sicknesses that needed nursing. But his nighttime troubles emanated from a different place altogether, the far-back marshland of his mind, dense with fevers and perseverations, offering up scenarios as fantastic as nightmares yet conscious, waking. Like God: What if God was not almighty, he thought, or even particularly effectual, but a loser, an underdog—kind and loving maybe, but outstrengthened by the forces of chaos and suffering? What if this world was simply the best He could do? Or the earthworms: so many of them that beneath the ground they must nestle together like the folds of a gigantic brain. And what would happen if that brain were suddenly to become conscious? And now the trees and their dry dead bodies. All his life, without thinking, he had allowed himself to be encased in their remains. Eaten at his wooden table. Walked across his wooden floor. Leafed absentmindedly through his books and his magazines. Blithely he had filled the hours with their boards all around him. In the daylight, the idea would never have bothered him, but now, as he lay in bed with the moonlight filtering through his blinds, his entire body hummed with apprehension. Suddenly he could feel the rafters looming above him, the walls bulking around him, and to his vision there came a swift progression of images: the ruinous machines that had severed the trees at their ankles, that had stripped them of their bark, drained them of their sap, and made a door of their ribs, and he, the dumb human specimen who had stepped unwittingly inside their corpses. What was the word for a house made of bones? A mausoleum. An ossuary. The cavemen had it right, he thought. You should find a hole in some cliffside and cower in it like an animal. That's what you should do. And now a worse thought: What if the trees had ghosts? And what if those ghosts came back for their bodies? It wasn't the first time, bundled under his covers with the lights out, he had sensed that he was not alone. Something in his groin tightened, and a pulse of ice ran through his veins, as the house settled with a creak against its foundations.

TWENTY

THINGS THAT FALL FROM THE SKY

Following the rain of ghosts, the earth smelled of moss and black pepper, and buildings appeared to waver at their boundaries, but then the sun came out, drying the puddles and lifting the dimpling marks from the soil, and the world seemed like itself again: untransformed. For a few weeks the city maintained its routines. The school bells rang at nine and four. The cars stacked up at the stoplights. On Saturdays the produce market busied itself by the river. It was easy to forget that morning when, without so much as a thundercrack, the air had filled with the spinning forms of a million dead spirits. Somehow no one heard the change say, I'm coming. Spring was beginning to turn to summer when the first trees yielded their crop of ghost-fruit. All at once there they were, a sea of soft-specked blue globes that bobbed from the tips of the branches, nearly irresistible to pick and, once picked, to bite into. When pierced, the skin produced a tiny leap of smoke. The flesh was not smoky to the tongue, though, but flossy and succulent. Raw, it tasted like an oddly nectary cucumber; baked, not like grapes per se, but like the grape additive in sodas and lollipops. Delicious. The seeds were as hard as BBs and had to be enucleated from a milky green cleft in the center, but otherwise the fruit seemed to satisfy the exact hunger it generated—to satisfy it perfectly. Soon after you ate one, though, it would happen: a door would swing open inside you, and through it would come drifting the specter of another person. To have a second identity nestling alongside your own, clouding around inside you and making your fingertips tingle, was invigorating but also disconcerting. Homebodies who had never traveled farther than the state park surprised themselves by talking about the crowded subways of Tokyo or the cave tombs of Sulawesi. Children complained that their spouses didn't love them anymore. A cashier at the ballpark recited a poem she insisted she had written in a language she said she didn't recognize. These additional personalities rarely lasted longer than a day or two, but everyone, to the last man and woman, was sorry to see theirs go. A life felt so much bigger with two sets of memories inside it. By November, most of the harvest had been consumed, most of the ghosts digested. By January, there was hardly anybody who had not become resigned to possessing one and only one spirit. But by March it was discovered that the BBs had taken root in the soil; by summer, at the edges of certain fields, they were growing into dainty saplings; and by September, the first hard blue kernels could be seen budding between their leaves. From then on, in at least this one city, people lived out their days with a sense of expansiveness and reverent mystery, nourished by this world and also by some other.

TWENTY-ONE

A STORY WITH A DRUM
BEATING INSIDE IT

A man is mowing his lawn in a state of perfect contentment. To every life there is a rhythm, he thinks, and as he strides back and forth laying bands of lighter and darker green in the grass, he feels that he has found his own. He marches behind his lawn mower the same way he marches through time, pressing ahead step by step, tacking resolutely from one week to the next, generating a steady pattern of lulls and accentuations. This is what life is like for him, and the correspondence between the greater rhythm of his life and the lesser rhythm of his yard-work, temporary though it may be, makes him feel as if he is not only at home in the world, but at home in it doubly. Here is one variation of him: its principal activity is mowing the lawn. And here is another variation of him: its principal activity is continuing to exist. Inside him the two variations are moving as one. Thus, his perfect contentment.

When he was little, as young as four or five, his father frequently permitted him to stand on the hipbones of the family's gas mower while he pushed it. He remembers riding toward the red house on one side of their yard, then the brown house on the other, the machine spilling long ridges of cut zoysia onto the lawn, and how the noise and the smell and the loco-motion invigorated him. The vibration of the motor caused an identical vibration in his body, and made his voice sound like a robot's. After the engine cut out, he would hear a thump like the thump of blood, but not in his ears, he thought: in the air, the sunlight, the soil. After a few minutes it would always go away. Back then his days bucked this way and that. By the time he started school, though, they had settled firmly into their rhythm. And the older he has grown, the more powerful that rhythm has become. Now, as he trims the grass, it seems as faultless as a song's. A car skims past. He waves at the driver. The sky is the color of an Easter egg dipped twice in blue dye. It is easy to believe that, behind or above it, the big empty spaces of the universe are as round and white and beautiful as an eggshell. At moments like this, plying between his driveway and his neighbor's, with the breeze on his skin and the sweat in his hair, he feels so good he imagines he will live forever. Not until the mower's engine stops does he hear the slow percussive thump he has heard ever since he was a child, so faint with distance and yet so tireless: the ghosts, in their multitudes, drumming at the walls of his life.

TWENTY-TWO

THE SANDBOX INITIATIVE

Eventually, when the planet began to cool again, thousands upon thousands of square miles of sand were returned to the seashores. Only in the most remote technical sense of the word could they be called beaches. They had, it was true, been abandoned to the land by the ocean, but no one wanted to visit, much less live on them, and so, littered with kelp pods and baby clam shells, they slowly dried up and seeded out, growing stiff little punk haircuts of grass. So rank and gray were these brine-soaked wastelands that even the gulls avoided them. What might have been valuable seaside real estate was instead a wilderness of sand, with no sea in sight. The question arose what to do with it all. In due course the president, at the encouragement of the secretary of the interior, signed Executive Order 58716, popularly known as the Sandbox Initiative. Until such time as the supply was depleted, it declared, every American family would be entitled to thirty-six complimentary cubic feet of ocean play sand, cleansed of bacteria and other impurities, with all its shells, bones, wrack, and pebbles carefully sifted out and discarded. A fleet of excavators was hired by the federal government to dredge the beaches, factories were built to dye and process the sand, and a vessel system of trains and flatbeds began distributing it to homes far and wide. Though the plan met with the usual hostility from the opposition party and was scoffed at by its pet editorialists, the property developers who were the real engine of the nation's economy greeted it warmly, offering the only ovation they had ever needed: a great huzzah of money. Industrialists and entrepreneurs purchased long sections of shorefront along the Atlantic and the Pacific, and piece by piece, as the sand disappeared, the land was graded, paved, and fertilized. By the time a year had passed, the coasts were blossoming with street malls and condominiums. The oceans were still receding, but they had been cleansed of the worst of their beaches, and, as a result, millions of sandbox squares had been placed in backyards across the nation. Most of the children who played in them, making their hills and moats, had never owned a sandbox before. If invisible fish occasionally muscled past them as they burrowed their fingers in the sand, or if they sometimes felt the ghostly prickles of crab legs tipping across their skin, well, they supposed, that was simply what sandboxes did. They were too young to guess—and the situation too novel for their parents to have taught them—that the sand had retained its memories of the ocean. And so they grew up as they imagined children always had, haunted by the tang of salt air and the blood sound of waves, which hushed, rose up, came to life, and hushed again.

TWENTY-THREE

RENEWABLE RESOURCES

The vice president of marketing at the major multinational petrochemical corporation is a slim man, and pale yellow like a wax bean. His collars bag at the neck, and his glasses lend his face an air of earnest intelligence that he feels he does not deserve. The other vice president of marketing at the major multinational petrochemical corporation is a voluble fellow, big in the chest and shoulders. He possesses a somewhat splenetic smile that he considers, despite all evidence, his most winning feature. Their salaries are roughly commensurate, their authority roughly equal, and each of them boasts a small cadre of subordinates who attend to their every word, but the first of the two vice presidents is responsible for fuels and lubricants, the second for textiles and specialties, and this, along with the promotion for which the two of them are competing, has made steadfast foes of them. How else would it happen that, after a few too many cocktails, they are standing on a bluff of black shale overlooking a neglected pine swamp, arguing quietly, viperously, in irritable thrusts and hisses?

It is nearly two in the morning, on the last night of the executive training retreat. All of the vice presidents' colleagues are if not asleep, then at least indoors. In a moment, after the splash, several of them will wake and peer outside, but they will not notice anything awry. Not until the next workweek will the secretary of the first man and the landlord of the second file a missing-persons report. One of the vice presidents says *nonrenewable resources;* the other counters with *energy density.* The first parries with *discretionary uses,* and the second retorts with *new frontiers of exploitation.* Then the great chock of shale on which they are standing makes a sound like the wind clapping into a sail and drops away.

At the bottom of the water, in a thick tomb of mud and seashells, beneath an eighteen-ton compress of rock, the two vice presidents will lie undiscovered for approximately seven million years. The first million they will spend waiting for their ghosts to depart from their bodies. By the second, however, they will have resigned themselves to the truth—that departing from bodies is not what ghosts do. From the third million through the seventh, the two vice presidents will slowly change. Their molecules will transform, their biota will vegetate, and they will feel themselves seeping crack by crack, sideways and upward, through a half-mile layer of sediment. For a time the swamp will have been an ocean of algae and plastic, but by the eight-millionth year it will be a meadow of giant reeds, growing high in the fernlands and mesas. From the micro-garbage of the world a new species will have emerged, capable, as humans were, of extracting oil from the earth. Only then, when the hydrocarbons that had once been their bodies are distilled, ignited, and consumed, will the ghosts of the two vice presidents be released, dispersing into the atmosphere and thus expiring.

GHOSTS

✦ AND ✦

TIME

TWENTY-FOUR

THIRTEEN VISITATIONS

The boy's irises were mismatched. That was what she noticed. One was a pale underwater blue, the other a brown so dark it commingled with his pupil. The woman had rounded the corner to find him sitting on her kitchen floor, playing with a small metal bulldozer. Probably she should have been frightened, or at least indignant, since she lived alone. He looked so vulnerable, though, with his legs spraddled out and his palm supporting his chin, that she leaned over and tousled his hair. "I think you picked the wrong door, buddy. What's the matter, you lost?" At her touch he gasped. Then he lit out toward the foyer yelling, "Mom! Mom!" No more than a few seconds passed before she followed him, but already the front door was closed and he was gone. Funny little guy.

Half an hour later she was fiddling with the coasters on her coffee table when the mushroomy smell of wet leather seeped suddenly into the room. A teenager came lumping past her in faded blue jeans and eroding tennis shoes. He switched on the TV, then caught sight of her and gave an electric leap. He flung the remote control at her. Her throat was so tight that the sound she produced came out in an alarming creak. That was when it happened—she could hardly have missed it—a little liquid detonation of a boy, erupting outward from himself like a bubble scattering apart. In the half-second before he vanished, she recognized something in his eyes: the left as brown as coffee beans, the right as blue as forget-me-nots.

Eleven more times that day he appeared before her and then dematerialized. A moment was all it took and *pop!* Each time she saw him, he was half a decade older—sometimes thinner, sometimes fatter, but always with those haunting eyes, brown and blue, and so unmistakably his own. Twenty, twenty-five, thirty, thirty-five, and each time perfectly at home. When she went to water the holly fern, he was sitting in a chair with a washcloth on his forehead. When she finished boiling her afternoon tea, he was rummaging through the ice cream in the refrigerator. When she decided to brush her teeth, he was trimming his sideburns in the bathroom mirror. His entire life was passing, all caught in the maze of her day. She watched as he put on a wedding ring and removed it and grew old. After a time, she was no longer frightened to see him, and to judge from the smiles he wore, he not only accepted but welcomed her. Shortly before midnight, she found him heaped at the end of the hallway, an old man, his arms bent like a kangaroo's. With a hard little kick of his breath he said, "You. I knew you'd come back. You're the reason I stayed here—stayed here in this house—never left—all these years of waiting and—" She placed a palm on his cheek. Already his lines were dispersing, and hers along with them, and in an instant she understood which of them was truly haunted, and which of them doing the haunting.

TWENTY-FIVE

THE OFFICE OF
HEREAFTERS AND DISSOLUTIONS

A genial middle-aged man, beginning to be old but with the same breezy disposition he had possessed all his life, received a letter of congratulations indicating that he had been accepted into the afterworld as a ghost. Attached to the letter was a bill for twenty-five dollars, payable by check or money order, using the enclosed courtesy envelope, to the agency of record. If anyone deserved such an honor, the genial middle-aged man felt, he did, so immediately he cut a check and made his preparations. At first the next world was a pleasure to him. The climate was temperate and the housing spacious. The other ghosts were ideally welcoming, neither too remote for his liking nor too meddlesome. Some eight days after he had settled in, however, another letter arrived, from the same agency, again requesting payment of the twenty-five-dollar processing fee. The genial middle-aged man was nearly certain he had settled this bill before he died, but his life had taught him that not every battle was worth fighting—the phrase was practically his motto—and since twenty-five dollars was only twenty-five dollars, and a bargain all things considered, he went to the bank and made out a cashier's check. Two months passed, during which he settled into his retirement routine of late-morning water aerobics and mid-afternoon hauntings. The third and fourth letters reached him simultaneously, bunched together in the same day's mail. One of them was recent, on letterhead reading "Talbott and Warfield Collections and Recovery." It warned that his admission to the afterlife would be revoked if the outstanding balance of his bill was not remitted promptly. The other was blighted with brown creases and bore a postmark nearly six weeks prior. It contained another invoice for twenty-five dollars, this time stamped PAST DUE and embossed and initialed by a notary. In red ink at the bottom of the page was a note instructing the genial middle-aged man to call a particular number as soon as possible. The woman who answered the phone seemed genuinely sympathetic. She blamed the confusion on a recent systems upgrade. In all likelihood, she reassured him, she would be able to clear his account with just a swift review of his vital information. And indeed, as soon as he offered his birth date, she stopped him with a proclamatory *a-ha!* "I see the issue. Someone mistranscribed the first digit of your birth year. Here, let me fix that for you." Inadvertently she tapped a three rather than a one, so that the official record of his birth suddenly postdated the official record of his death by almost a full millennium. At that moment, and for the next thousand years, the genial middle-aged man ceased not only to be but ever yet to have been.

TWENTY-SIX

AN OBITUARY

The minute that elapsed between 9:05 and 9:06 on the morning of Sunday, December 20, 2015, did not simply recede into history, as was traditional. It died. Such a situation defied all precedent. Suddenly time, which had always been continuous, had a gap in it. For the next sixty seconds it seemed as if the whole giant edifice of chronology would crumble and fall. Its uppermost layers began shelving and swaying, and a disjointed crackling sound arose from their perimeter. But then 9:06 drew to a finish, tocking neatly into the cavity left by 9:05, and in the long succession of minutes that constituted the past, yet another assumed its place. After that, time proceeded as it always had, albeit with a short delay at the conclusion of each sixty seconds. An hour still lasted an hour, and a day a day, but along the way came an ongoing series of almost imperceptible lulls, briefly supervening whenever the past overtook the present. Now the flow of time had a subtle friction to it, as if a bead had gone missing somewhere along the link. The change was mild, just a tiny new inflection in the temperament of being, but gradually, to those of us who remembered the way things used to be, it became apparent that something in the fundamental character of existence had been altered, if only subtly. There was a wooziness to life, a pliability. Prior to 9:05

on the morning of Sunday, December 20, 2015, reality had been all spruceness, regularity, and order. Afterward it was looser, more yielding, lengthening and contracting as one by one the minutes filled their vacancies. It moved forward like a practiced drunk, disguising its fitfulness as grace. Again and again it settled into itself, again and again let down its guard. Once upon a time, time had preserved its balance. Now, instead, it achieved it—a speck of a difference but a difference nonetheless. Maybe that was what it was or maybe it was something else: the spirit that had sifted from 9:05 in the final instant of its final attosecond, taking with it everything that had just finished happening, and taking it not into the past, as time had always done before, but into the hereafter. At 9:05 and three seconds, a meteor had flashed in the skies over the mid-Pacific. At 9:05 and sixteen seconds, the lone flower of a species that held the cure for cancer in its petals had been crushed by the blades of a trencher. At 9:05 and twenty-four seconds, a landslide in eastern Turkey had revealed the bones of an ancient settlement, before, at 9:05 and thirty-eight seconds, a second landslide had reburied them. At 9:05 and fifty-nine seconds, the latest wave in an infinitude of waves slid serenely back into the ocean. Now all that was gone and no more. If the world had become a slipperier place since then, more wayward and less trustworthy, maybe it was just the ghost of that dead minute, rising up and attempting a possession.

TWENTY-SEVEN

THE MIDPOINT

That man in the rain-spotted peacoat, with the cigarette and the woolen cap, whose dockworkerly appearance is mitigated by his spruce goatee and his natty shoes, is growing older in both directions. From the fixed point of his birth he has been maturing not only into the future but also into the past. The first of these conditions he shares with most—perhaps all—of his contemporaries; the second, as far as he can tell, with few—perhaps none—of them. He was in kindergarten before he realized that the bidirectionality of his life was something out of the ordinary. One day, through carelessness, he shattered a porcelain vase that had been in his mother's family for generations. Why, he wondered, was she so angry? After all, right there in the past, on the same walnut table into which he had just tossed his backpack, the vase was still intact, wasn't it? But she spanked him anyway and sent him to his room. "A hundred and fifty years," he heard her complaining to his father, "destroyed just like that." She gave something less than a laugh: a snap of the voice, gone at once, like a firecracker; and instantly, with that something that was not quite a laugh, the man in the rain-spotted peacoat's eyes were opened. His mother was not like him. His father was not like him. Not everyone performed their aging both forward and backward.

As the years went by, he watched the people around him grow both older and grayer and younger and spryer. He was envious, sullen, haunted by a sense of misfortune. He himself was not growing younger in either direction, only older into the future and older into the past. Wave by wave, as he tuned in to the same TV shows they did, saw the same movies, endured the same elections, he felt his elders becoming his contemporaries. At ten he had twenty years of life to his credit—ten counting forward and ten counting backward. At twelve, he had twenty-four. At twenty-five, he caught up to his parents. At forty-eight, he overtook his grandparents. Now, he supposes, at fifty, he has a full century of existence to his credit. And this, the man thinks, taking a draw on his cigarette, is the signal fact of his life: the time he considers *his,* and that he understands directly, by having experienced it, is effectively double that of everyone else. Some nights he lies awake reflecting on the precipitousness of it all. Each year seems swifter than the one before. He finds the acceleration alarming. In the end, he imagines, his ghost will burst from his skin like a pair of rockets, racing forward and backward into the darkness. Once there was eternity in all its stillness. Then, with his birth, came a sort of fragmentation, through which time began to flow. And eventually, at his death, he thinks, there will once again be eternity, but eternity in a torrent, a gush, eternity picking up speed.

TWENTY-EIGHT

THE WHIRL OF TIME

The ghost resided in a country full of clocks. Some of the clocks were trees, methodically adding rings to their trunks. Some of the clocks were breezes, marking out a moment or two by ruffling the grass or churning the curtains. And some of the clocks were people, their hearts pumping out the seconds. Behind the entire living world was the drum of time passing, and silently, from his gap in the air, the ghost listened as it rushed along. He had been a ghost for as long as he could remember, ever since an enormous pain he could barely recollect had ended his life in the mud and the rain. Since then, from his perspective, the years had gone by in a ceaseless barrage, replacing the generations just as swiftly as it created them. Children became parents and grew old and took to their beds, and then the beds were empty. Streets, fences, buildings, and monuments crumbled and melted back into the earth. Who could possibly keep track of it all? Who would try? Ghosts are meant to fix themselves to one particular house, meadow, or street corner—to select a place and *haunt* it. It is this tenacity of attention that keeps them from coasting through the centuries like herons over water. But this particular ghost had never developed the knack for standing still, so the material world meant less and less to him. Eventually, when the clocks of everything became too loud in his ears, he resolved to bring his flight to a stop.

First he chose a dwelling to haunt, a small post-and-beam house on a hill beside a market square. The whirl of time took it down, though, before he could steady himself there. Next he chose a person to haunt: a young teacher instructing her first geometry students. He had hardly shown her his countenance, though, before she retired and was bones in a graveyard. Houses were too ephemeral, he decided. And people were like raindrops. Finally he chose a stone to haunt, one of the oldest and most immovable in the city. Gradually, through an effort of will, he was able to move beneath its surface. A stone keeps its own time, and soon enough, haunting it, the ghost did, too. To his relief and surprise, the time he found himself sharing with the stone was less precipitate, more measured. From the crack in its side he watched the flicker of the seasons slow. The fields stopped boiling with flowers. The clouds began to cotton the sky. It was cool and quiet inside the stone. After a while, he ceased to hear the ticking of the trees, grass, breezes, and hearts. Whole days and nights went by when he forgot he was a ghost at all. He imagined he was only the large brown mass of granite resting imperturbably in the city park. The stone where the bugs no longer landed. The stone that the children no longer climbed.

TWENTY-NINE

MINNOWS

At first he failed to understand his predicament. To become a ghost upon dying was one thing, but to become a ghost centuries before you were born was something else entirely: a fate for which his imagination had simply not prepared him. There was the present, and on one side of it was the past, and on the other side of it was the future. Overhead was the sky, the sun, and a tissuey curve of moon. At the horizon a cliff peak stood ringed in white clouds. Time and space, he thought. What a hodgepodge. Luckily, the ghost was resourceful, with an intelligence that was, if not swift, then at least tenacious, digging and poking away at whatever questions the world offered up to him. So, by a kind of intuitive census, he took stock of his situation. This was how he saw it: the body to which he would one day belong was, for the moment, separated into billions of distantly arrayed molecules. Some of those molecules were enlisted in other animals, while some were jacketed inside fruits, grains, flowers, herbs, or vegetables. Most were washing around in various far-flung belts of the ocean. A few, of course, by the law of percentages, were somewhere nearby, but from what the ghost could tell, they added up to no more than a freckle-on-an-arm's-worth—not a body, or at least not much of one. Gathering them together, the ghost decided, would be futile. His only real option was to rally his patience and wait. Eventually the man who was destined to yield him up would be born and then die and the ghost could take his place. Very well then, he thought. He would set off into the centuries. Not far away a stream was trickling over a bed of shale and yellow clay. The sunlight was drawing bright tangles on the surface of the water, and a shoal of minnows was drawing bright tangles beneath it. From the long grass on the bank, the ghost extended the part of him that was practicing to be a hand. He wondered, as it pierced the surface, if the minnows would make a hole around it. All at once the light on the water seemed to impress itself inside him. Then, with the suddenness of a thought, he was gone. The universe had corrected its mistake. Six hundred and eighteen years would pass before the ghost returned, and eighty-one more before the body that contained him stopped functioning and he was set free. It would be male, that body, portly, slightly professorial but also slightly military, with back trouble and dry skin and the smell of soap hovering about it—the most intimate possession of an almost entirely ordinary man, one whose sole oddity, dating to his infancy, was the feeling that he had been alive much longer than he could have been, or than seemed possible.

THIRTY

A STORY SWAYING BACK AND FORTH

Summer followed spring, and autumn, summer, and that was the end of it. For a week, maybe two, the trees displayed their glossiest oranges and reds, but the leaves never brittled or fell, only swayed slightly, like brushtips. Flocks of birds made nets of themselves in the air, as though preparing to migrate, but as the sun set they dispersed back into the treetops. Night after night half a moon shone in the sky. Then, just when October was supposed to tumble over into November, the leaves refilled with chlorophyll, the days brightened, the temperatures rose, and another summer arrived. The river of time was flowing backward. Spiders retracted their silk, pumpkins drained into their stems, and the clouds drank up the gullies. First the world went sliding back through October, then through September and August, until a shimmeringly hot afternoon in the middle of July when, over the course of an hour or two, while the bugs made their reverse shrilling sound, time gradually lost its wind, decelerated, paused and turned back around. Suddenly the days began moving forward again. There they went, the spiders, clouds, and pumpkins, making webs, spilling rain, and plumping out on their vines. Each minute followed the one that had come before, until, once more, the first of November approached and everything slowed down, stopped, and doubled back on itself. Time was not a river after all, it seemed. Time was a pendulum. For a few months it traveled in one direction, for the next few months in the other. The trees regreened and then reyellowed, the sun journeyed east and then west, people grew a little older and then a little younger. Some of them died and, dying, became ghosts or became nothing, but then their bodies reassembled and came back to life. With each swing of the months, however, the curve of time diminished slightly. It reached from late July to mid-October, early October to early August, September the 1st to September the 15th, *swish swish swish swish,* until finally, in a little series of converging agitations, it stopped altogether. Time was not a river. Time was not a pendulum. Time was a plumb line. At one minute past three on Friday, September the 8th, it fell still. Everything ceased changing. Bonfires turned to sculptures. The waves made sawteeth out of the ocean. This—this moment—was where eternity would take place, not in the glow of paradise, and not in the blackness of oblivion, but in a stillness charged with memory and premonition.

THIRTY-ONE

A TIME-TRAVEL STORY WITH A
LITTLE ROMANCE AND A HAPPY ENDING

The stories the girl with the penny loafers favored exhibited a particular shape. They were time-slip stories, simple and trim, about girls like her, with penny loafers—dreamy, earnest girls who experienced time travel in its purest and least complicated form, unmixed with science and untroubled by paradox. They had no doodads or rocket ships, these stories, no great machines with beams of light or circumvolving halos, only a little magic. A portal, a spellbook, a ghost, even a knock on the head would do. The mechanism made no difference. It was the slip in time that mattered: the feeling that, with just the right nudge, you could wake up inside your life but outside your moment, with people who knew you were remarkable but could not pin down quite why. Somewhere long ago, the girl liked to pretend, if only you could find your way there, you would experience an improbable but passionate romance, so deeply fated that it would surmount any barrier, "even," the book's covers often promised, "time itself." The heroines of these stories, the stories she loved, were always between the ages of fourteen and twenty-one. They had long red hair, like she did, and hazel eyes, like she did, and they ventured, by accident, into the past rather than the future. Sometimes they came back to the present, but never deliberately, and never permanently, because the past was where they truly belonged, and by the final page, without fail, they would find a way to return there. Their adventures always involved a love affair that seemed doomed but was in fact merely complicated, with a man (or adolescent) who had hair that was black like India ink, and blue eyes with an ice in them that just the right kiss—*her* kiss—would turn to water, and a forbidding manner that hid a sweetly husbandly (or boyfriendly) vulnerability. And a happy ending: that was important. Though a desperate beginning was important, too. In the best of the stories, at the conclusion of the first chapter, after it had been established that behind her odd, almost antique shyness, the girl was extraordinary and deserved much more love than she had ever been given, she would step through a door while wearing her penny loafers, and all at once the light would feel different to her, the air. She would discover that the coins had transported her to an earlier year: to 1978 if they were stamped 1978; 1925 if they were stamped 1925; 1932 if they were stamped 1932. The dates had to match—that was the rule. Only by replacing the older pennies with current ones could she return to her own day. This was why the girl who read the time-slip stories always wore the same tight-fitting penny loafers. She wanted to be ready. Sooner or later, in her heart of hearts, she knew she would encounter a door that was not just a door but a small disruption of reality. And she wouldn't think twice.

GHOSTS

✦ AND ✦

SPECULATION

THIRTY-TWO

THE PHANTASM VS. THE STATUE

His name was the Phantasm; his power, to move discontinuously through space. Most people, he liked to explain, advanced through space along an unbroken line, interval by interval, but he, the Phantasm, *retroceded* into space, as if through a thousand tiny holes, then emerged from behind it again, either nearby or far away. It had not always been so. Growing up, he had moved through space like everyone else: by walking, running, occasionally bicycling or roller-skating. But ever since his days as a young subnuclear scientist, when a trillion-to-one accident bathed him in a torrent of lambda radiation, he had come and gone from space instantaneously, like a ghost. Accordingly, he had become a superhero. Not the most formidable superhero, he had to admit, nor the most effective, but a superhero nonetheless. The problem was that in order to progress from place to place, he had no choice but to use his abilities, vanishing from one point and reappearing in another even if the location to which he was traveling was only a fraction of a millimeter away. When, for instance, he wanted to flip a hamburger, he was required to disappear from his position beside the grill and rematerialize in a position that substantially overlapped with it, one in which little to nothing had changed except for the angle of his hand and the spatula—

upended, the both of them. In order, however, to maintain his grip on the spatula and ensure that the blade remained underneath the patty, he had first to pivot a single degree or, rather, to issue from space at a point so close to the one from which he had originated that the arrangement of the handle in his palm showed only a single degree's disparity, then a second degree's, and then a third degree's, until he had successfully overturned the spatula and along with it the patty—so many incremental motions, so rapidly achieved, that to an outsider he must surely have looked like an ordinary man, flipping a hamburger with no superheroics whatsoever. Alternatively, if he chose, he could travel across the world in the blink of an eye. His archenemy, the Statue, was a victim of the same subnuclear accident that had created the Phantasm, but unlike the Phantasm, the Statue moved through space inflexibly, adhesively, to all appearances not at all. On his concrete plinth he stood with the same air of straight-backed malevolent boredom he had displayed ever since the lambda rays overtook him, surveying parks and bazaars, college quads and cemeteries. His powers immobilized any person careless enough to touch him. No one but the Phantasm could set those people free. Once, and only once, had the Phantasm come into contact with the Statue himself. The Statue activated his superpowers, the Phantasm activated his, and all at once the two of them, archenemies, found themselves together in the spaceless everywhere of the underverse, that strange blizzard of electrons that lay between all places, where no point was different from any other. For that bare instant, neither of them could have said which of them was stationary and which was in motion, nor which the hero, which the villain.

THIRTY-THREE

FOOTPRINTS

This story is a parable. You may have heard it before. Once there was a man who was part giant, part ghost, and part magician. So remarkable was his enormity, so strange his otherworldliness, and so profound his mystic ability that those who knew of him fell to their knees when he came into sight, trembling and hiding their faces. Around him swirled waves of worship, fear, and adoration. The world would have been his toy if not for the fact that he lived in a constant state of antagonism with himself. After all, he thought, how mysterious, really, was a magician the size of a fortress? How menacing was a giant who passed harmlessly through walls and fences? And didn't spells and enchantments demean a ghost? The problem, he believed, was that he was one person rather than three, or three inside of one. This indivisibility, it was a burden. This terrible gumminess of being. And yet, for all his power, there was nothing he could do about it. He should have been three great men, and instead he was a single tri-part man, irredeemably damaged and compromised. The thought of it, the imperfection, stung at and bedeviled him. Again and again over the long years he attempted to wrench himself in three. The more frustrated he became, the harder he struggled, but though his exertions ravaged everything around him, to his body they brought only sweat and bruises. The part of him that was a magician traced symbols in the air to cast out the part that was a ghost, recited incantations to raise up and unfasten himself from the part that was a giant, but this was one spirit he could not dispel, one mountain he could not lift. Instead, if only by accident, he stripped trees of their branches, hefted boulders into lakes and hillsides. The part of him that was a giant battered at his chest and yanked at his limbs, trying to beat out the ghost and the magician, but in his clumsiness he only toppled schools and barns and churches. The part of him that was a ghost twisted one way and then another, hunting for some doorway out of his body, but the cage of his bones was far too tight, and all that sprang loose were his rage and desire, which blew from him like an awful wind, tearing down forests and dividing rivers. So it was that the man who was part giant, part ghost, and part magician wandered the earth in his agitation, trying desperately to cleave himself in three. He cared for nothing else. Behind him along the shore of his life, as far as the eye could see, stretched three sets of footprints, and wherever they passed lay obliteration and ruin.

THIRTY-FOUR

PASSENGERS

By the time the spaceships arrived, a series of microorganic accidents had stripped the earth of life, leaving only the bare rocks, the ashy water, and a throng of human ghosts. The aliens spent little more than half a morning exploring the planet's surface before they entered the record in their log—"no signs of life"—and departed. They were several solar systems away before the second assistant engineer noticed a small reality imbalance in the lead vessel's structural field. He was loath to risk the hectoring of the first assistant engineer, his all-too-predictable insults and comminations, for what was probably, after all, just a diagnostic glitch, so he sent a query to the fleet's thousand-some sub-engineers, asking whether their scans had detected anything unusual. Immediately the responses cascaded in: "Ship 0113 is point-six degrees off the reality standard," "Ship 0272 is reading a spike of eleven—no, make that twelve units in our nonbeing metric," "Ship 1091 here. We've got some kind of wave malformation in our tangibility drive," and then, from Ship 0837, "Oh, no. What's happening? They're coming from the floors, the walls, they're everywhere."

The second assistant engineer was not reassured. With each message, the traffic of unlikelihoods increased: power losses and temperature drops, pounding and rasping noises, fainting epidemics. Seeing no alternative, he left to report the matter to the first assistant engineer, who contrived as usual to blame him for the chaos. "Molecular distortions! Authenticity blurs! You'll fix this and you'll fix it now, or so help me, I'll yank every antenna from your head." Though the second assistant engineer attempted to defend himself, he had little time to formulate his reply. He had squeaked out only the most tentative "Sir" before a hollow buzzing noise passed through the air, the sealing panels detonated from the walls, and a thousand dark forms flowed wobbling into the room. From outside the door came screaming, moaning, the sound of breaking equipment. The rest happened more rapidly than anyone could have predicted: the pools of ice and shadow, and the captain's evacuation order, and then the second assistant engineer slithering alongside the first assistant engineer through a dozen narrow hallways of airborne debris until the two of them reached an escape pod, which dropped at once through the dilating lips of an ejection portal, joining the thick litter of other spheres the fleet had jettisoned into space—ten thousand bobbing life capsules. The stately silver vessels that abandoned them to the vacuum were not empty, not exactly, but from then on the crew that haunted their cabins was bodiless, wistful, and only half real. At last mankind had reached the stars.

THIRTY-FIVE

NEW LIFE, NEW CIVILIZATIONS

By the twenty-fourth century, the question had been answered definitively: transporters did not in fact convey a person, bodily, from one place to another. They killed him and replaced him with an exact duplicate. The new question was whether the copy, like the original, was endowed with a soul.

A team of researchers was appointed to resolve this mystery. They located a subject who had never, in all his life, availed himself of a transporter—no easy task at this late stardate. "Do you certify that neither you nor your component molecules have ever been reconstituted via teleportation?" Never, the subject agreed. "Do you understand that, once beamed through subspace, though you will perceive yourself to be indistinguishable from the person you have previously been and therefore continuous with him, you will in fact be a re-creation, and may or may not possess a soul?" I do, the subject consented. These preliminaries accomplished, the subject was scanned, his metrics catalogued, and the researchers escorted him into the transporter lab for the test. The inaugural phase went off without a hitch. The subject was energized, a frequency shimmer filled the room, the subject materialized on a nearby platform—check, check, and check. But a close comparison of the initial and subsequent scans revealed an anomaly. The copy of the subject, the researchers discovered, did indeed possess a soul. It was the original who did not. Perhaps there was a malfunction in their diagnostic equipment. Over the next several weeks, though, taking all due precautions, they tracked down and tested eighty-three additional subjects, from sixteen separate planets, transporter virgins every one. In each case the result was the same. Whether the subject was human, Saurian, Vulcan, or Betazoid made no difference. Inside the replicas: souls. Inside the originals: no souls. It was unexpected, indeed most perplexing, but incontestable.

The report the researchers issued to the Federation numbered roughly six hundred pages, most of them purely technical, as befit the parameters of their assignment. In a half-page addendum, however, they offered two notes of poetic conjecture: (1) If, as some argued, voluntary teleportation could be considered a form of suicide, had they discovered evidence that suicide, in at least this one form, might result not in losing your soul but in gaining it? (2) If, as now seemed likely, the invention of the transporter some 180 years ago had generated the first souls in an otherwise soulless universe, had Heaven come into being along with them; or had it been waiting all along, a grid of empty golden streets whisked with light and gentle breezes, since the first men rose from the dust and the clay?

THIRTY-SIX

A BLACKNESS WENT FLUTTERING BY

In the end, as it transpired, the engineers could not prevent the barrier from collapsing, and the explosion, when it arrived, was even worse than they had anticipated: formidable enough to destroy not only the core galaxies but the universe itself. Of that gentle, orderly cosmos, home to so many magnificent minds, only a ghost remained. It lay spread across the light years, a vast spectral emptiness powdered here and there with deposits of oscillating particles. These "planets," these "stars"—they barely deserved the name. One might have mistaken them for matter if not for the compactness of true matter; the matter, that is to say, of the actual universe, the perished universe. For the fact was that the eruption had taken with it not only the celestial plenum but everything that once filled it—the warmth of space, the indelibility of the senses, the supernal pulse, the outer strand: all of it. To be a ghost, it seemed, was to undergo a great transposition. Where there used to be light within you, the ghost of the cosmos thought, suddenly there was darkness; and where there used to be darkness, pinpricks of light. In your innermost depths, where the celestial melody once resonated and sang, you generated only a faint thermal hiss, impossible to ignore, so maddeningly persistent that it kept you from resting or falling asleep. What else was there to do in your wakefulness but catalogue what you had known and lost, along with the few frail substitutes that had replaced it? So you made an inventory of your comets, your novas, your black holes, your constellations, the galaxies that quivered with a sensation of turmoil and unease, the photons that flickered with exhaustion. After a time, with so little rest, you did not even know what you were anymore. That's what it was like, the universe reflected: you failed to recognize yourself for what you were, a ghost, and believed you were a living being, the cosmos itself, the real thing. Maybe in your cells there lingered a dim awareness that long ago, in the indeterminate past, you had been something other than what you now were—something better, more real, amazed by the bounty you contained—but no matter how close you came to the truth, it continued to elude you. Only occasionally, for less than a moment, did you recollect yourself as you used to be. Then the memory faded, and you resumed counting your planets, your stars, and the few sentient beings, on one world or another, who, like you, supposed they were alive, and who spent their days telling all the wrong stories.

THIRTY-SEVEN

THE PRISM

It was meant to be a sort of cosmological prism, a lens through which they could view the universe dispersing into its thousands of parallel possibilities, but when the scientists powered it up, it didn't work. Nine years of labor and hundreds of millions of dollars, wasted! The project's director stalked around the armature of the machine like a hyena circling its prey. "This dumb damned broken thing," he said, and launched a kick at it. The discharge from the transformer killed him instantly. Later, reviewing the lab recording, his team watched the whole grim episode in slow motion—the director yawing around to fire his leg out, his cheap plastic shoe melting off his foot, a corona of sparks wavering above his head—but then, when they scanned the secondary footage, taken through the lens of the prism, something else: his ghost leaving his body. "A ghost," they called it, and a ghost it unmistakably was, the classic Halloween kind, all transparent drapery emanating from a featureless white globe, like a lollipop wrapped in tissue paper. It leapt from the director's chest and vanished into the ceiling. Several months passed before they obtained permission to transport the machine to a penitentiary and aim it at an inmate who was receiving a lethal injection. Sure enough, at the very moment the EKG stopped tracing its pinnacles, a ghost could be seen fleeing the poor man's body. Hypothesis, prediction, experiment, conclusion. They had not invented a cosmological prism; instead, it seemed, they had invented a window into the spirit world. Yet afterward, examining the footage, they saw something very strange: one of the guards shedding a ghost of his own. He was locking the execution chamber when his knees wobbled and he brought a hand to his chest. He did not die. Even so, a ghost came spilling out of his body. The next week, in the lab, the camera accidentally captured an intern stumbling over his ankles. He came inches from cleaving his head open against the edge of an aluminum cabinet, but did not do so. He had, in fact, already regained his balance by the time his ghost sprang loose. So then: a new hypothesis. The prism was capable of observing not merely the one *actual* death of a person but the thousands of parallel *possible* deaths. With every icy sidewalk crossed, every heartbeat skipped, every near miss on the highway, you expelled another ghost into the atmosphere. Imagine how many billions of them there must be. Trillions. Surely from outer space, at any given moment, the world must be bristling with ghosts like a porcupine.

THIRTY-EIGHT

HIS WOMANHOOD

A cognitive scientist, long-limbed and handsome though sad to say bald, developed a method by which to stimulate the neural centers responsible for presentations of masculinity and femininity. His technique was neither invasive nor dangerous, and when he discovered that his assistants were meeting in the lab after hours to employ it recreationally, what, he decided, was the difference? Why not join them? They fit the device to his bare head, adjusted the dials, and triggered his masculine plexus. All at once the brilliant young cognitive scientist felt ambitious, decisive, and blunt. He stretched his shoulders, flexing his trapezius muscles until he heard his spine crack. When someone—Avery, he believed the name was—mentioned that the science center used to house a charter school, he did not say, "I never knew that," but instead, "I must have forgotten that." Avery, Jordan, Kelly, Parker, and Robin: the cognitive scientist had just arranged their names in alphabetical order when the device was recalibrated to trigger his feminine plexus. He experienced a mild itching sensation, and then, in an instant, felt nurturing, patient, and a little sheepish. He worried that he had been tactless, that Avery (who was the most sensitive of his assistants, after all, and whose name, besides, was Jamie, he now recalled) had perceived him as cavalier or dismissive, just a skosh rude perhaps. Should he apologize? he wondered. He caught himself rubbing the collar of his shirt between his fingers. The cotton was beginning to pill. Then the gender excitation equipment shut down with a surrendering hum, and his assistants removed the device from his temples. How instructional, the cognitive scientist reflected. It appeared that the barrier between manhood and womanhood—or at least *his* manhood, *his* womanhood—was not a chasm but a seam. It barely existed at all. In the weeks that followed, however, his womanly qualities did not abate. The cognitive scientist might be drinking his coffee or checking his phone when suddenly, without warning, some Mrs. or Ms. would come tiding up inside him. Hello, he would think, it's *you* again. His usual grayness or brownness of feeling kept giving way to strange brilliances of sadness or pleasure. At every sniff of jasmine or lavender, or, oddly, pumpkin pie, he felt a small pang of sensual longing. Clearly the neurostimulators had awakened something inside him. He set off to discover what it was. It took many years, several hundred discarded hypotheses, a cancer scare, a religious conversion, and a spur-of-the-moment palm reading before he began to suspect the truth: that while his mind was a man's, his soul was a woman's. The two of them, his mind and his soul, had achieved a sort of marriage, he mused, though whether death would mark its divorce or its consummation, only time would tell.

THIRTY-NINE

THERE ARE PEOPLE, THEY HAD LIVES

Because the first afterlife had become too crowded, they built another. A team of laborers and engineers was dispatched to the marshes that lay beyond the celestial border to siphon the mud from the bogs, fill in the bottomlands, and stitch the earth up with green grass and brown sod. From the remaining marshwater, they created crystal-clear lakes with beds of white shingle. In no time at all, sightly new neighborhoods of houses, parks, and tennis courts were assembled on the shores. As a finishing touch, a pedestrian bridge, curved like a bass clef, was erected over the largest of the reservoirs. The mosquitoes still presented a problem, so the whole area was blanketed with insecticide, after which the problem was the *ghosts* of the mosquitoes, legions of wailing specks needling around on pure dumb instinct. But, as the chief engineer pointed out, even the finest developments had their headaches, and if phantom mosquitoes were the worst of theirs, they could count the project a transcendent success. The team packed up its equipment and returned to the main office. The afterlife job, they reported, was finished, under budget and ahead of schedule. All it lacked were its residents, and such a dilemma was hardly a dilemma at all, since the living, say what you would about them, kept dying. More ghosts arrived by the day, and from then on nearly all of them were assigned to the second afterlife, with its clusters of decorative bulrushes, its plazas paved with red and yellow bricks, and its smart new houses that smelled of paint and sawdust. In addition, to alleviate the congestion, it was decided that the population of the original afterlife would be reduced by roughly four percent. A lottery was conducted to select the several billion requisite emigrants from the first afterlife to the second. Some of the administrators worried that this would leave people thinking of themselves as either winners or losers—that those of them whose names were called would feel cheated of their rightful homes, or, conversely, that those of them whose names were *not* called would feel cheated of some grand adventure. Yet no one foresaw what has actually happened, which is that everyone feels cheated now, everyone like a loser. In all but the most trivial ways, the two afterlives are exactly the same: the trees bud, the breezes blow, there are people, they had lives. So perhaps it is just human nature that the ghosts in the first afterlife spend their time feeling neglected, obsolete, as if the world has outdistanced them, while the ghosts in the second spend their time swatting at insects that whine and that buzz but that cannot feed on them no matter how hard they try.

FORTY

THE SOLDIERS OF THE 115TH REGIMENT

Often, in their fear and excitement, the soldiers of the 115th Regiment saw the bullets flying as if in slow motion, all that metal as thick as rain in the air, yet coasting, gliding. How easy it was to imagine themselves strolling across the battlefield like tourists, brushing the tic tac of lead from their uniforms, lost in another world. Yet among the bullets was something else that came and went almost imperceptibly: discharges of light, both beautiful and horrifying, that cut blinding patterns into the air and then vanished with an incredible swiftness. These calligraphies of light were amazing to behold, yet also sickening somehow, abhorrent. They were only visible at all because of the way the world was barely moving, and even then for less than an instant. The soldiers were reluctant to discuss them. It seemed dangerous, sinful even; deranged. Surely only the most shameful Section 8 cases saw mazes, zigzags, and falling stars of light making formations of art inside a barrage of gunfire. One afternoon, though, after a few rounds of liquor, the men began confessing their visions to one another. "Have you ever noticed—?" "Yes, yes!" "By God, I've seen them, too." The second rifleman was convinced that the patterns were angels watching over the front. The machine gunner suggested that they might be maps of a kind, forecasts, tracing the paths the bullets would follow. They reminded the mortar operator of those openings in time and space that decorated the cover of *Amazing Stories;* doorways, he said, to Mars, or to the deep past. Finally PFC Matthew Kostial muttered something about the scientific method, and then, in notes as round as a tuba's, announced drunkenly, "Learn by doing, buddy boys. Learn by doing," and set off into the bullets. No one who watched him stumbling over the field in slow motion could forget how, just before he fell, the air fractured around him like the glaze on an old painting.

Though their memories could not quite reproduce the cracks of lights that had encompassed Private Kostial, some trace of the pattern must nevertheless have incised itself in the soldiers' minds, for occasionally, years later, the radio operator would see lights where they did not exist: on riverbeds, in the concrete he was pouring, in his sock drawer. Now and then the antitank gunner would detect something in his wife's handwriting, or his secretary's—a strange design that emerged like a fog from behind the letters, seeping briefly into view before the paper reinhaled it. And the artillery mechanic confounded generations of high-school orchestra students with the eccentricity of his baton-work, certain that with just the right sequence of gestures, he would summon the ghost of the private from the battlefield and he would step out of the light, whole again, bringing the scent of cordite and booze to the stage.

GHOSTS

✦ AND ✦

VISION

FORTY-ONE

ACTION!

That famous director standing at the edge of the railway concourse is determined to make a movie that is, as they say, literally unwatchable. Seventy-one, and garlanded with more
honorary doctorates and lifetime achievement awards than he
knows what to do with, he again feels like the wild-haired punk
filmmaker of his enfant terrible days, whose work *Cineforum*
so memorably dubbed "the wreck not only of the art world,
but of art, and of the world." Once again he has a purpose.
The movie he is preparing to film will, he believes, constitute
his single greatest achievement—if, that is, it is, as he hopes,
literally unwatchable. By "literally unwatchable" he does not
mean a movie that is bad or distasteful (or at least not per se;
not unwatchable for those reasons). Nor does he mean a
movie that is incompetent or maladroit; in fact, the very opposite. No, the movie he intends to make will be "unwatchable"
in the strictest possible sense of the term: because it genuinely cannot be seen. Now, there are several ways in which a
movie that cannot be seen might be said to be unseeable. (1) It
might not exist, or might exist only notionally: as an idea or
a thought experiment rather than a series of moving images.
But the famous director considers such subterfuge beneath
him. (2) It might be shot, processed, or shown in such a way as

to prevent its own observation—for example, using film that records only ultraviolet or infrared light; or projected onto a small screen several miles distant, or a high screen several miles in the air. The famous director regards these options as one-offs, art installations, and not the kind of honorable proletarian filmmaking to which he has always aspired. (3) It might be unwatchable not because the medium itself forbids observation, but because no one remains to do the observing. Imagine, for instance, a movie documenting the release of a toxin that, over the course of six or seven weeks, while the footage is in postproduction, will cause the swift and cascading annihilation of all life on earth. Theoretically, the only gamble in such a case would be the classical one: that is, whether people are transfigured into souls, ghosts, upon dying—and therefore, at least ostensibly, capable of watching a movie—or whether they are discharged into the blackness of oblivion. The famous director is, as it happens, in possession of just such a toxin. He stands at the edge of the busy concourse, beneath the boom mic and the tungstens, and mops the sweat from his brow. The camera is rolling. He pries the top off a capped glass vial. It produces the tiny, almost humorous, champagne-bottle sound that children make when they pop their fingers from their mouths. In no more than seven weeks, if he has gambled correctly, the movie the famous director is shooting will be ready for viewing and yet unwatchable, the perfect capstone to his long and innovative career.

FORTY-TWO

THE WAY THE RING OF A MOAT
BECOMES COMFORTING TO A FISH

A particular man woke up one day and, from then on, saw the same face on everyone he met. He was riding his co-op's elevator when it began. Two women joined him on board, their features so precisely alike that though they entered at separate floors and did not greet each other, he supposed them to be twins. At the fifth floor the elevator collected a third woman, identical to the first two right down to the sand-colored mole on the knifeline of her left cheek. Triplets? But the cabbie whose taxi the man hailed wore the same face. As did the gentleman who ran the bagel cart at the corner, the bicycle courier who was balancing himself at the crosswalk, the mother who was tugging her child across the street, the child whose hand she was tugging, and everyone else the man saw, not only during his ride to work that morning but all that day and for the rest of his life. The face in question was feminine, lightly freckled, with a square chin, an elliptical hairline, lips that quirked naturally to the left, and eyebrows that were darker toward the nose than toward the temples, traits that lent it a misleadingly testy expression, as of someone who found even the happiest moments of life mildly disappointing; or someone happy, perhaps, *to be* disappointed: who had finally been disappointed in exactly the way she had always expected to be. The expression vanished instantly when the face went into motion, which was how the man knew that it was misleading, but since most faces, most of the time, are not in motion, he could not help perceiving the face he kept encountering as crabby—albeit proudly, almost delightedly, so. At first, in this new version of his life, the man found it hard to shake the feeling that everyone was irritated with him. Eventually, though, he grew used to the expression. Faces— *all* faces—greeted him with a look of ghostly pique. It was simply a fact. Once he accepted it, the ubiquity of the sight became almost comforting. The woman who peered out at him from other people's faces seemed incapable of disguising her bitter amusement—and so, having been seen by her, he felt bitterly amusing. Knowing that salesclerks would invariably be bitterly amused to run his credit card, priests bitterly amused to offer him the sacrament, dentists bitterly amused to fill his teeth, gave him a sense of security. Sometimes he wondered about the face's original owner—the prototype. Who was she? Would he recognize her if they met? Had they *already* met? Increasingly, as the years went by, he came to view her as a kind of wife, uniquely related to him, the one person in the world who might find her face less exotic than he did, or more, in either case because it was her own.

FORTY-THREE

SPECTRUM

A reclusive art lover, fond of Matisse and Cézanne but with a lifelong inability to distinguish his reds from his greens, purchased a pair of glasses that were said to remedy color blindness and discovered at once that the world was quivering with hues he had never seen before: a thousand amazements of color. The most pitiable thicket of roadside trees suddenly revealed a riot of emeralds and golds to him. Beneath the clay of their skin people flushed with pastels and peaches. He spent a spellbound Saturday at a traveling Monet exhibit, marveling at the pink petals of the blossoms in the paint, the mottled blues and greens of the lily pads. A week went by before, due to a software error, the manufacturer sent the reclusive gentleman a second pair of the same glasses. Rather than packaging them back up, he decided he would conduct an experiment. He went to the Museum of American Art, found an empty bench, and stacked the second glasses neatly on top of the first, adjusting the lenses carefully over his eyes. Was he foolish to be excited? Perhaps. For all he knew, though, an entire missing spectrum was waiting to be discovered. He readied himself for the strange new pigments he was imagining to erupt into being—silvorange, vermillow. Instead, what did were ghosts. In this spot or that, scattered around the room, a dozen configurations of light smudged the air. When one of the configurations opened her mouth as if to yawn, he realized what he was seeing. There beneath the Eakins a ghost stood scratching the side of her nose. There by the Beckwith another sat loosening his collar, prying it from his Adam's apple with an impatient two-fingered tug. Standing in front of the Redmond, a ghost in a beaded gown was clasping her hands to her chest like a convert clasping a Bible. Around him the gentleman saw almost as many ghosts as non-ghosts. His optometrist had explained that the color-blindness-correcting glasses worked by modifying the wavelength of the colors that reached the eyes. Maybe the spirit world occupied such a wavelength, too, the man thought, and by wearing both sets of glasses at once, he had altered it just enough to make it visible. In any case, nearly every painting was adorned with some rapt spirit. He recognized in them an attitude very much like his own— the attitude, that is to say, of art lovers, holding their faces not with an inquisitorial tilt but perfectly upright, at ninety degrees, so that they could view the canvases dead-on. Their world was a gallery—*this* gallery. It was the kind of place that had been familiar to him ever since the third grade, when Miss Terrell took his class on a field trip to the Children's Museum. Had there been ghosts surrounding them even then? Yes, he thought, probably so. And now, in their presence, it struck the reclusive gentleman that for all their furtiveness, all their detachment, they had been with him for most of his life—the only life he had, he thought, though not the only life there was.

FORTY-FOUR

EVERY HOUSE KEY, EVERY FIRE HYDRANT,
EVERY ELECTRICAL OUTLET

She was a difficult child to manage. Not difficult in the way of most two-year-olds: she slept soundly enough, enjoyed her baths, was careful with her toys, and kept her socks on her feet—and as for her appetite, it was almost indiscriminate. Even the meals she initially rebuffed she could be persuaded to reconsider. However, she cried inconsolably when she saw the headlights of certain cars approaching, refused to toddle past the tree in the yard without kissing the bare spot on its trunk, and seemed personally affronted by electrical outlets, swatting at them with her palm and demanding "No! Stop!" before backing distrustfully away. And about those rejected meals: sometimes she would clamp her lips closed when offered a plate of food, tucking her chin disdainfully into her bib, but if you stirred the ingredients, or even just rearranged them a little, she would wolf them down. What she was thinking it was hard to know, since she lacked the vocabulary to explain herself. No color was so bright and no noise so conspicuous as the submerged reality her senses seemed to present to her. The problem she perceived, but was incapable of expressing, was that, arranged just so, a hot dog, a lump of peas, and a dollop of creamed carrots made a face, and she couldn't see a face without imagining it was inhabited. And, of course, she was right. The objects of the world pressed up against the barriers of their faces, staring out of them in dumb captivation. Every chest of drawers, every sneaker tread, every cigarette lighter—everything with the suggestion of two eyes and a mouth—hosted a secret visitor. Those visitors were the ghosts of the dead, who had no features of their own and therefore borrowed the faces of pot lids and wood knots to peer out at the living. They watched them argue and kiss, cook and bathe, read and exercise and sleep side by side. If only people understood how tedious the afterlife could be, the ghosts thought, how starved a spirit could become for motion, activity, fizz, transformation, maybe they would do something better with their lives. The faces never spoke to the child, never even varied their expressions, but she understood that they were there, awake, watching, and responsive. Some of them she tried to comfort, while others she hid from or spurned. How was she able to guess what lay inside that mute host of haunted objects? you might wonder. But that isn't really the mystery. The mystery is how she decided which of them she was going to love.

FORTY-FIVE

THE WALLS

Once, in this very house, there lived a man who papered his walls with photographs. His object was to cover every available sliver of wall space, laying picture beside picture until the bare white plaster had become an ocean of faces. Each day he added a few more to the mosaic, using little strips of double-sided tape. Squaring them into place was not just an urge for the man but a mysterious imperative. The people in the photos were neither his friends nor his family members. They were not even his acquaintances. They were, to the one, strangers. And maybe that was the point. The man who papered his walls with photographs did not want to be surrounded by the people who knew and loved him. He did not want to pretend he was precious—not to anyone. He wanted only this—for his little life to pass as if in a crowd of strangers. Accordingly, every Saturday, he made the rounds of the city's flea markets and estate sales, exhuming handfuls of photos from shoeboxes, scrapbooks, and envelopes. The process he had adopted was leisurely, intuitive, and idiosyncratic, but also in its way inflexible and weirdly choosy. His preference, though he could not have explained why, was for old matte Kodachromes from the sixties and seventies, the kind that must have had some cream to their colors when they were first developed but that now, with age, were reddening, imperfecting. He rejected professional portraits, or even deliberately posed stills, in favor of candid snapshots. Accidents. Couples waiting accidentally for restaurant tables. Kids splashing accidentally in wading pools. Ordinary people who had been accidentally captured making accidental faces in accidental settings; thousands of them, tens of thousands, in an accidental reliquary of halides and light. How many of them were women; how many men? How many were smiling, how many frowning, and how many wearing some other, more equivocal, expression? The numbers kept changing. He had trouble keeping count. Every time he attempted a survey, it seemed that more of the strangers were staring directly into the room at him, their retinas returning the burst of some long-expired flash as though they had been startled out of their activity like animals. The man began to suspect that he was visible to them, and visible not only from the surface of the walls but from somewhere deep behind them. The strangers could see him. They could *see* him. He was the flash, he himself, a living, breathing discharge of light. Year by year his collection grew. The closer he came to completing it, the more he sensed that he was witnessing a consummation of some kind, a finishing touch. He wondered how many of the strangers had died in the years since their pictures were taken. Most of them? All? One day, he thought, he would be among them, another small astonished phantom from the accidental past, his red eyes shining through the walls at the living.

FORTY-SIX

PLAYTIME

One: Stay inside after dark. Two: In daylight, keep to the fields and the plazas. Three: If you see the shadow of a person without the body of a person, do not cross its borders, for it is a ghost. These were the rules the people of the village observed, though they might with more accuracy have been called alarms, admonitions, warnings, so grave were they, and so pregnant with consequence. Even the most gentle and loving of parents smacked, shook, and spanked them into their children. Accidents, nevertheless, happened. Take the girl trapped right now in the glade beyond the village border, who is waiting for the sun to go down. In her fourteen years, she must have seen the shadows of a thousand ghosts, scissory gray shapes that have appeared on the walls of buildings or the dirt between one house and another, vibrating with an expansive scorn. She was only three the day a neighbor of hers was seized by one of them, and she still remembers the horror of it: a man in blue overalls misstepping into a wandering shadow, then his shout as it transformed him, or consumed him, or whatever it was that ghosts did to leave a heap of clothing where a body had been. She knows how to evade the ghosts when the sun is shining. She knows how to flee indoors when the evening comes. The problem is her dog, a rambunctious black-and-white spaniel, all tail and skull and ears, who puffs and barks at the door whenever he judges himself deserving of a walk. He is a rattle-brained little thing and she loves him, which is why, earlier that afternoon, when he spurted off into the woods in pursuit of a squirrel, she let her instincts get the better of her. Without thinking, she went lunging in after him, grasping for his leash as it snaked through the undergrowth. The light fell here and there through the foliage. Ranks of black trunks rushed past her like fence posts. Before she knew it, he was gone with a startled yelp, taken by what had seemed to be the outline of a maple on the ground, and there she was, deep in the forest, holding his leash and collar. By luck, she had staggered to a stop in a patch of sunshine, but the trees around her laid down a maze of shadows, far too many for her eyes to disentangle, and the danger of venturing back into them sapped the strength from her legs. What could she do but stand at the center of the clearing, willing herself to take a few steps every ten minutes or so, as the patterns of darkness the branches made in the dirt slid slowly, excruciatingly, toward the east. Not far away, gathering at the edges of the glade, were dozens of holes in the likeness of bodies. At dusk, she knows, the sun will paint their shadows in long black stripes to the horizon. Eventually their borders will become impossible to distinguish. We call this night. The ghosts call it playtime.

FORTY-SEVEN

ALL HIS LIFE

Forget dinosaurs. Ghosts were the coolest. They could turn invisible. They could pass through walls. And best of all, they haunted people. Let the other kids stomp around the playground making claws and roaring like T. rexes. He would rather moan and rattle his chains. "What," his teacher asked him one day, "is with that starey, ummy thing you're always doing?" And he responded with a deep-down ghost's creak: "I have returned for you, Ms. Kathleen, with a message from beyooond the graaaave." His tone was so ominous that she backed away, shivering electrically. Yes, nothing could top a ghost.

He was in such a hurry to become one that before the year had passed he was ninety and lying on his deathbed. His throat was way past speech, his ears way past hearing, but as his breathing stopped, and then his heartbeat, something began to sway before him like the fumes from a charcoal grill. Gradually those fumes became a face. It smiled warmly at him, that face, a memory from some forgotten cradle dream. When a voice said, "Rejoice! For your drifting has come to an end. The next life is waiting to welcome you," he understood every word. Clearly his ears had found their power again, and so, it turned out, had his mouth. He asked the question he had been preparing for as long as he could remember: "Is this the spirit world?" Then came the reply: "No, not the spirit world. The *other* world. Behold." It was not a tunnel of light he saw but a thousand overlapping tissues of it, foam-white and silver. With the barest pressure of his mind, he knew, they would part for him and absorb his years, his pain, washing his life away as they had the lives of so many others. The light shimmered with peace and music, a strum of transcendent well-being, sighing *rest in me, rest in me.* But that wasn't what he wanted. It never had been. And when the murmur in his ear said, "Come, my child, follow me," the answer he returned was instantaneous: "No thank you." The voice cautioned him, "Do not be hasty. Those who cling to this earth are doomed to linger here. It is a dreary, bitter, aimless existence, a ghost's." But "All the same . . ." he said, and turned his face away. Once the light had dimmed, he realized he was back in his hospital room, not inside his body but hovering over it. He slipped through the ceiling and then through the roof. Outside, all around him, were more lost souls, bobbing in the air like jellyfish. Since that time, he has floated through the gray limbo of the afterworld, filled with a vindictive joy, searching out the most timid and frightenable of children and appearing in the dark at their bedsides. It is so awesome.

FORTY-EIGHT

TAKE IT WITH ME

He liked to say that the blue of the sky was so lovely he was going to take it with him when he died—and when the time came, he did. The ghosts whose numbers he joined had always dwelled in a world of flat grays and pallid whites. Noon to them was nothing but a whiter twilight, midnight a darker dawn, but now look: here and there, around and above them, in sheets, parcels, crisscrosses, and dashes, a fine and lustrous blue. It was in the breast feathers of the pigeons, the braiding on the surfaces of ponds, the glaze on certain pieces of pottery. Everywhere they turned there was another touch of blue in the gray, and with each glimpse of it, the ghosts felt a little more alive. Maybe their skin was only a memory of the skin they used to wear, but still it seemed to tingle. Maybe their hearts were only lace and fog, but still they seemed to beat. Was this what it had been like, their lives? Why hadn't they noticed?

Hardly a week had passed before a woman died carrying the red she had always loved from the blooms on her daughter's cheeks. Suddenly, alongside the blue, were the warm speckled petals of spray roses and the blush marks on apples and peaches. Next came the green of olives, then the softer green of grasshoppers and raw coffee beans, then the rich, almost black, brown of good soil and dark chocolate. A little boy brought the glossy yellow of the boots he liked to put on when it rained, an old man the ruby red of the dice at his favorite casino. A lepidopterist contributed the distinct theatrical purple of the boomerang shape—or at least that's how it looked to her—that crested the wings of the luna moth. Soon only a few stray patches of white and gray remained in the hereafter, and death by death, as just the right ghosts arrived, these too were painted in: with the heathered blue of shirts and scarves, the jupitered orange of Easter eggs, the bright yet milky pink of the sunrise a man once saw on a clear April morning from the deck overlooking his backyard.

Meanwhile, in the world they had left behind, which is to say ours, the sky was no longer blue and the trees no longer green. Instead, where the colors used to be, was only a thick snow of toneless particles.

FORTY-NINE

A STORY SEEN IN
GLIMPSES THROUGH THE MIST

Nothing much had happened in her life, but the little that had was more than enough, and though the landslide that flattened her car was the most of that little she had ever experienced, she was pleased to discover, upon emerging from the wreckage, that she had entered the afterworld, where the nothing that happened was even less. The country of the dead, her explorations revealed, was almost entirely empty. There was, of course, herself—or at least the ongoing chain of associations and impressions she chose to continue calling herself. And there was some element of being or half-being against which she was able to enact her identity. But no matter how far she wandered, she found no one else, only a sparse background of fogs and vapors with just enough detail to remain vaguely familiar: a mist of houses and a haze of streets through which her spirit moved like a ripple of air. Eternity, it transpired, was desolate, unoccupied, a place where everything that was was barely anything at all—and, as such, as much of her as anything could be. She could hardly imagine a better fortune. She had always been a person of ticklish sensibilities, easily overcome by the ordinary frictions of life. The lighter the brush of experience, the more keenly she seemed to feel it, and now fate was offering her a world free of disruptions and vexations—free because there was so little world to it, and so little, therefore, to be vexed or disrupted: just a few scattered essences, as intangible as shadows. As a ghost, she was able to tuck herself into the spaces between these essences, and soon, with practice, into the absences between the spaces. The problem, she eventually ascertained, was that the less of everything there was, the greater the portion of it anything would occupy, as a result of which the most inappreciable movements were like bedlam to her. Every so often something in the nothing would lap or quiver or stir, and in her senses everything else would diminish, the way late at night, in an empty house, a cricket can sound like a symphony. So it was that the afterworld, which, if it had been like no Heaven she had ever been promised, had nevertheless been a kind of Heaven, became instead, though like no Hell with which she had ever been frightened, a kind of Hell. In her quiet little nook of the grave, even the least of something was the most of anything.

GHOSTS

✦ AND ✦

THE OTHER SENSES

FIFTY

A LIFETIME OF TOUCH

Visiting the cave temples of Ellora in the final year of his illness, the famous sculptor noticed that the breasts of the female statues gave off an aqueous sheen, as if dipped underwater. When he asked why, the tour guide explained to him that more than a dozen centuries of male caresses had anointed them with palm oil. "You understand a carving not only with the eyes," he said, gesturing ecumenically. "You understand it also with the hands. Please, please, go ahead, my friend." This exchange, which lasted only a few seconds, would determine the artistic trajectory of the rest of the sculptor's life. Standing before that rock-cut basalt, he set himself the task of creating a statue so irresistible to the hands that, given a thousand years, every inch of it would be glossed by admiring touches. As soon as he returned to his studio, he began experimenting with blocks of soapstone. The statue would be a woman, he decided, and therefore, to him at least, innately enticing, but he wanted its desirability to be both more extravagant and less specific than that: an object that combined the carnal allure of a beautiful woman with the structural allure of a geometric solid. Two months into his work, as a test, he sprayed his half-dozen strongest attempts with a UV aerosol whose properties were activated by skin moisture. In the gallery where he displayed his sculptures to the public, he posted a sign that read PLEASE TOUCH. That night, after the doors were locked and the lights dimmed, he examined his statues with a mercury wand. The bluing appeared in jellylike patches, concentrated mainly on the breasts and hips. The difficulty, he realized, lay in devising a female shape that was not only *tempting,* but so *uniformly* tempting that whatever contact it attracted would be distributed evenly over its entire surface—the breasts, yes, but also the elbows, the knuckles, the spine, the armpits. The vertical cleft between the nose and the lips. The bumps of cartilage along the superstratum of the ear. Following another few months of trial and error, he calculated that the ideal size for such a statue was eight to twelve percent larger than the average woman, the ideal posture the straight legs and slight upper acclivity of someone leaning in to smell a high-set flower. Most appealing of all to the hands were those statues he displayed not on a pedestal, or even at ground level, but in a shallow basin. The idea violated every supposition of what he had come to think of as his craft, but there it was, shining in blue, the irrefutable evidence. He was preparing to make the switch from soapstone to marble when his illness finally caught up with him. In an instant, rather than sharpening his chisels, he was la-de-daing through the afterworld, one ghost among millions of others. The ghosts had been nestled for so long inside their bodies, and held there so tightly, that they shone now like lanterns. For thirty or sixty or eighty years they had been embraced by their own skin. The famous sculptor was mildly piqued to realize that he would not complete his masterwork, but consoled to observe that he too was shining—polished, he now perceived, by a lifetime of touch.

FIFTY-ONE

THE RUNNER-UP

All his life he had maintained a distinct ambition: to be the second-greatest composer in Vienna, that minor talent whose flame would be first enfeebled and then subsumed by someone else's genius. To achieve such a goal, he knew, would take a lifetime of labor. He was no older than nine when he set out to write a series of competent but indifferent melodies for the clavier and the violin. By adolescence he had graduated to unmemorable short sonatas for the organ and piano, and later, as he grew into his abilities, to humble keyboard concertos that, one of his teachers exalted, "had at best their modest charms." He worked unflaggingly, and his standards were high. Now and again, dampening some stray line of inspiration from a score, he imagined he felt a phantom hand guiding his pen: a guardian, a muse, an angel. The music was so clear to him. He listened in as the strings extended their apologies to each other while the flutes and oboes offered their own little *pardon-me*s and the drums coughed spasmodically in the background. If only he could capture the sound he heard, he knew even the most indulgent listener would find the result vaguely but inevasibly disappointing. By the time Emperor Joseph II offered him his first commission, he was producing symphonies so consummately mediocre that they were forgotten by the public almost immediately, dirtying the air for a moment and then sinking away like the froth the waves deposit on the sand. The tepid applause they received never failed to delight him. Even the occasional bravo could not dismay him much, for nearly always, he had learned, given a performance or two, it would be balanced out by a countervailing jeer. He was confident that if he continued to exert himself, his compositions would gradually worsen. What he did not anticipate was that the genius whose magnificence shone so bright before him, that gentle conductor whom God had surely ordained to his work, would be outshone by a greater genius still. A pale young twig of a musician arrived from Salzburg, debuting his talents before the emperor, and all at once the Salieri whom the composer so revered was faced with a Salieri of his own, which meant that the minor composer who longed to be the second-greatest in Vienna was, at best, the third Salieri in the chain. Presently he understood how remote his ambitions had become. One day, he thought bitterly, when the history of composition was written, it would show only an infinite succession of diminishing Salieris, each one drearier than the Salieri that had come before.

FIFTY-TWO

SO MANY SONGS

It was bound to happen sooner or later: the world had run out of new songs. "I'm surprised it took *this* long," the missus said. We had been around for the best of it, she and I, with Elvis shading over into the Beatles, and doo-wop into Stevie Wonder. Even back then, in the AM days, folks sensed that it was too good to last. Must have been a week or so ago the two of us were having one of our Monday evenings, cooking pasta as we listened to Hot 101—"Always the latest, always the hits"—when the DJ announced that it had finally arrived, the last possible song, and the station would now cease broadcasting. A few ticks of microphone noise, then nothing. Static whispered from the speakers like tires on a concrete highway. *Hoosh-sha. Hoosh-sha. Hoosh-sha.* It was long and straight, that road. Went stretching on for days. Well, the missus and I continued to tune in whenever we stood at the chopping board or the stove. Habit, I suppose. But still it was nothing but *hoosh-sha, hoosh-sha.* Washing lettuce one afternoon, she listed her head to the side and asked, "Do you hear that?" I humored her with my let's-pretend nod, but there was nothing let's-pretend about her expression. "Vexed" is the word I would use. She swatted my arm and impatiently, gesturing at the radio, said, "That," and then *"That"* again. At first all I could make out was the familiar road-hum of static, but something was swelling there, something that wanted to be heard. Gradually my ears became attuned to it. Ghost music: that's what people are calling it. It's music from somewhere else, no question. Music without the need for bodies, if that makes sense. No melody, no form, hardly any development, just a faded sense of time and how it burgeons and leaks away, as if all the songs that have ever been born and died have been born and died the way water transforms into steam. Alive, they expressed themselves in surges and sways, and now, dead, they express themselves in breaths and hisses. Occasionally you might detect the shimmer of some earlier tune through the mist, but never for very long. You can't move to a sound like that, can't dance, but you can relinquish yourself to it, and that's what they've done, my missus and so many others, in dusty sofas or cars stalled out in driveways. All that first evening she stood in the kitchen listening to the radio, and again the next morning, and now, whenever I go looking for her, that's where I'll find her. Deaf to my voice. Deaf to damn near everything. Each day her stance is a little more peaceful, her eyes a little more colorless, her skin a little more translucent. Last night I dreamed she had gone floating out of her dress. A ghost of herself: that's what she was. My plan is to reach my hand out and touch her. And soon enough—just you wait—I'm going to try it. The small of her back. That's my idea.

FIFTY-THREE

A MATTER OF ACOUSTICS

Ghosts, like giraffes, are usually silent but sometimes hum. Solitary by custom, and famously melancholy, they cluster occasionally in groups of two or three, to all appearances by accident rather than design. Let the smallest gap remain between them and they will preserve their silence, but they are mist, not flesh, and move by flowing out of themselves. When the shapes they have adopted cross or intermingle, they produce a deep centrifugal thrumming tone, like high-tension wires resonating in the wind. To call such noises speech humbles the word. There is nothing organic, much less human, about them. Call them instead propagations of sound. These zingings and moanings seem to embarrass the ghosts, as if anything other than the most solemn hush, of the kind dust adopts, or stones, was a failure of manners. Given the least opportunity they will part, and their humming will cease. Along with it, however, will cease the only obvious evidence of their existence, for it is not ghosts themselves that the living perceive—not the spectacle of ghosts, the aura of ghosts. It is the acoustics of ghosts. And therein lies the problem. In an age such as ours, so hungry for the transcendental, most people desire *more* spiritual encounters rather than fewer. Out of this desire, and the ghosts' reluctance to fulfill it, has arisen the profession of spectral engineering. The principle is simple: the isolation ghosts favor is gravely tranquil—not the wilderness seclusion of the ancient prophets, all tempests and proclamations, but organized, chosen, metaphysically suburban. The job of a spectral engineer is to coax the ghosts out of those suburbs, as it were, and into the city. Certain features have been found to channel them effectively together: curving walls, sunken exits, corners where wooden pendants clack. Others repel them: salted windowsills, rooms painted the color of blue water. A spectral engineer will lay such places out in careful succession so that the ghosts who cross them must, unavoidably, intersect and therefore hum. When this work is done well, a house may be described, with no misadvertising, as "haunted"—and haunted not as a result of occult forces or vague spiritual restlessness but traffic engineering. For the ghosts, it is true, such methods might produce some discomfort, but if so it is surely no worse than the mild vexations rush-hour commuters must endure. Moreover, any such distress is temporary, theoretical, and subject to interpretation, and should be measured against the happiness of the living—the homebuyers—whose desire for the immaterial and the supersensible lies beyond all doubt. The ghosts are free, having overlapped, to return afterward to their isolation, where they may think whatever ghosts think, sequestered from each other by the neat picket fences of death.

FIFTY-FOUR

BOUQUET

She knew that when he died his voice would die along with him, yet somehow she had failed to recognize that his scent would die, too. Oh, it lingered for a few months in the clothes he left behind, but then it shrank away and she had yet another extinction to mourn. One afternoon, though, as she stood in the kitchen unbagging the groceries, it reappeared: the unmistakable incense of his body, earthy and sweet, like the flat spice of modeling clay. It rose up powerfully around her—*whoom:* like that. For an instant, before the facts of her life overtook her, she expected to see him fossicking around in the cabinets again for a jar of peanuts or a bag of chips. Foolishness. So much foolishness. She turned back to the refrigerator, transferring the last of the eggs to the egg cradle. That night, though, as she lay drifting off to sleep, she detected his fragrance once again. In her delirium she was convinced that he was bending his limbs into their bed, trying to arrange himself under the covers without disturbing her, but her awareness was no more than the thinnest haze, and soon not even that, and when she woke the next day she remembered only a small tickle of scent in her nose and a brief feeling of familiar warmth. In the morning it happened twice more, first while she was checking the news on her laptop, and then while she was brushing her teeth. And then once more a couple of hours later, when she went to the door to sign for a package. Over the next few days, the same dense mixture of aromas found her again and again. Time after time, in one room or another, something in the air would shift and a great exhalation of fragrance would engulf her. She concluded that it was his ghost. He couldn't talk to her, couldn't make himself visible, but from the other side of death he could offer his bouquet of chemicals, that scent which had accompanied him through a hundred thousand doors, into a lifetime of business meetings and dinner parties, each burst of it a sign that he still existed, and not only existed but existed nearby. She began to resent the wool musk of the carpet, the sweet leather smell of the couch. To ignore them took the dedication of a penitent. Ignore them, though, she did. He had found a way to communicate with her, and she wanted to communicate with him in return. When he was alive, he used to tuck his face into the dip where her neck met her collarbone, breathing in the jasmine and vanilla of her perfume, the bergamot of her body lotion, the bell-pepper tang of her sweat. The solution seemed obvious. The next time she noticed his presence, she stood in front of the box fan and let it carry her aroma into the air. For the next eleven years, until she died and he took her away, that was how they spoke to each other, her scent and his scent making the scent of them together.

FIFTY-FIVE

THE MUD ODOR OF THE
SNOW MELTING IN THE FIELDS

The house is different this morning, of that he is certain, even if, by "different," he is not sure what he means. Slightly too full: that is the best he can do. Everything seems to be brimming out of itself like beer foam. He himself, by comparison, feels flatter, filmier, less real. It is a sensation he associates with dreams, though he is confident he is not dreaming. You can't smell in dreams, for one, and the house smells the same as ever: a shifting potpourri of grocery-store paperbacks, bath soap, cooking oil, and hamper must. No, he has to admit, to his usual senses the house is completely unchanged. It is only to his *un*usual senses that it is different. If pressed to describe the difference with a single word, he would say that it is ampler. The house is ampler. It possesses a supersaturated quality, a lavishness; an overdyeing, he would like to say, except that it is not the ink of things he is detecting, not the color or even the appearance, but—but what? Way back in the darkness of his mind he feels a little caper of intuition. He pauses. In his blundering, he must have gotten something right. Overdyeing. Supersaturated. Ampler. His unusual senses. Maybe that's it, he thinks. Maybe the difference is not in the house but in himself. His senses. The logic seems sturdy to him, even impeccable: if everything looks the same to his eyes, and sounds the same to his ears, and smells the same to his nose, but is *not* the same, then he must be using something other than his eyes, his ears, and his nose to detect it. For reasons that are shadowed in obscurity, he possesses a new and mysterious sensory apparatus, one that can perceive, as if by nervous induction, the ampleness of things. There by his front door leans the ampleness of an umbrella. Here in the dining room stands the ampleness of a wine rack. There in his study sits the ampleness of his desk, and on that desk rests the ampleness of a lamp, and beneath that lamp spreads the ampleness of a magazine. Everything swells with the plenitude of its being. Only he, and he alone, does not. By the time he returns to his bedroom, he believes he has steeled himself for what he will find. He is convinced that he is prepared. And in fact it is not the sight of his body, still radiating warmth on the bed, that so disquiets him. It is the realization, gradually dawning, that he is capable of exhibiting a sense to which he does not register.

FIFTY-SIX

INSTRUMENTOLOGY

That gentleman in the fifth row of the auditorium, listening as the orchestra consonates its instruments, is only half himself—the spiritual half, to be exact. To call him disembodied would be, if not exactly false, then at least, he thinks, misleading. He is *negligibly* embodied, grazingly or *obliquely* embodied, reposed as he is within the intermediacies of his material half—a thin gentleman in an English suit who is, like him, waiting in the fifth row of the auditorium for the symphony to begin. Simultaneously, in precise soldierly concert, the two of them, one half material and the other half spiritual, cross their legs, twiddle with the loose button on their suit jacket, inspect their wristwatch and prod at the bridge of their eyeglasses. Each of these motions occurs at the will and instigation of the gentleman's material half, as has every other motion in their long, pinched, snug and inseparable life. The truth is that the spiritual half of the gentleman feels that he is the material half's prisoner, though he acknowledges that the material half can hardly be blamed for this situation, since he is only dimly conscious that his spiritual half exists, and, even if he realized otherwise, what, short of dying, could he do to emancipate him? Immediately next to the spiritual half of the gentleman, toying with the clasp on the spiritual half of her leather clutch, is the spiritual half of his girlfriend. Directly in front of them is the spiritual half of a tall adolescent with a stiff posture and a tumbleweed-like mass of hair, the material half of whose head is blocking the harp and a few of the violins. And two rows ahead of that boy and a few seats to the left is the spiritual half of the gentleman's ex-wife, wearing the spiritual half of the good blue dress he bought her shortly before he announced he had fallen in love with someone else and was leaving. She has always been vindictive, his ex-wife: vindictive, exacting, and shrewd. The spiritual half of the gentleman in the fifth row knows all too well how much she would relish his discomfort. As such, he is hoping to go unnoticed by her. If he could will himself not to cough or raise his voice, he would. But, as always, his behavior is not his to choose. He is subject to the decisions of his material half, who often comports himself—and therefore him—in ways he finds embarrassing. Striking matches on his thumbnail. Sneezing with an actual "ah-choo." That sort of thing. Tonight of all nights one might think he would know better, but the fellow is rather dense, and sure enough, as the conductor takes the stage, he begins applauding with a meaty clap, far too loud for the occasion, as though taking pleasure in the great boom his hands produce. Surreptitiously people turn to get a glimpse of him. It is just the latest of the many times the spiritual half of the gentleman has wished in his humiliation that he could smack his material half on the forehead. Oh, for the day when his spirit will be divided from his flesh. Oh, for the day when they can go their separate ways.

FIFTY-SEVEN

WHEN THE ROOM IS QUIET,
THE DAYLIGHT ALMOST GONE

A ghost, through no fault of his own, found himself trapped inside a living body: an infant's, to be exact. Over the eons he had heard rafts of legends, parables, poems, bromides, stories, jokes, and songs about hapless spirits who, caught in the snare of a body, were yanked out of the herebefore and into the corporeal world. The moral was always the same: your task was to endure. Simply that: to endure. The infant you had become would ripen into an adult and waste away, and in a century or so you would be free. The ghost had traversed half an eternity's worth of centuries already. Doing so had never presented him with any particular difficulty. To say so was not immodesty on his part, only frankness. He had a proven ability not only to exist but to continue existing. What, he told himself, was one century more? And with that thought, the ghost settled into the body as if into a sturdy hammock and prepared to while away the decades. Soon, though, to his dismay, he discovered that his situation obliged him not only to pass the time but to *experience* it, in full and without distraction, his attention fixed carefully on each fleeting moment. Otherwise his ghostliness, his selfhood, would slip away from him and his existence become irrecoverable. At first the life within which he had become enmeshed was all milk-drunk afternoons and curtains twirling in half-open windows. He believed he might survive it, if only barely. But one day, during his third year of captivity, when the body that had trapped him was crunching an ice cube made from orange soda between its back teeth, the strain of the ghost's vigilance began to wear on him. Deep inside himself he felt a warning twinge. When, he worried, would this intimation of pain and inattention turn into the thing itself? The question so bothered him that he nearly lost his presence of mind. From then on the ghost was forced to be on constant guard against himself. In his fifth year, while the body that contained him was making whip noises with a stick it had found in the yard, a momentary daze swam over the ghost, an absentmindedness he corrected just in the nick of time. In his twelfth year, he developed a persistent ache that caused his senses to tremble. At twenty-five he began experiencing groundswells of intense fever and nausea; at thirty-two, a tireless ringing noise. The body that was imprisoning him went on aging. Never once, as far as he could tell, did it notice his distress. He found it hard not to trace his difficulties, setting off after them the way a cat does a butterfly. Sometimes it was not until the very last second that he reasserted his self-control. Midway through the forty-third year of his imprisonment, to his horror, as the body that had trapped him was racing across a racquetball court, the ghost noticed the wringing sensation of its muscles tightening around him. With barely an *oh, no*, his vision blurred and he felt himself falling unconscious. For all anyone knows, he is falling there still.

FIFTY-EIGHT

A SORT OF FELLOW

That fellow working at his teeth with his tongue is hardly a fellow at all. He exhibits few of the necessary attributes, neither wholeness, nor dimension, nor materiality. In fact, he possesses only a single characteristic: the near certainty that on the lower left side of his mouth, embedded between his first and second molars, is a particle of food he cannot dislodge—a sesame seed, maybe, or a fragment of peanut. Until recently this characteristic of his belonged to an elderly reference librarian. Following a short illness the librarian passed away, whereupon his ghost, or rather the ghost of his conviction that some smithereen of food was stuck between his teeth, came into being. Where the rest of the librarian's qualities have gone the ghost cannot say. To other ghosts, presumably. He has no idea. The fact that he himself is a ghost is not yet within his grasp, much less that he is one ghost among many. For now he is no more than that single aforementioned property: the impression that something is caught between his teeth, possibly a seed but most likely a nut, and impossible to expel without some dental floss or a toothpick, however rigorously he might employ his tongue to the purpose. This, for better or worse, is the essence of his personality. Around it, one grain at a time, a bit from this person and a bit from that, the rest of him will gradually accrue. Next to arrive, from a waitress killed in a highway accident, is the opinion that what they call country music these days is not country music at all but pop music with a twang and too much cologne. After that, from a tenured economics professor, comes a bold, almost defiant sentimentality about house pets, such that he can hardly bear to watch a movie in which a cat or dog is endangered, even a goldfish, without closing his eyes and covering his ears. From a successful real estate agent he inherits an awareness, somewhat pained, of the swiftness of time; from a skilled radiologist, a preference for swimming pools over lakes and rivers. One by one the qualities gather themselves to him. The dapperness of a fry cook in his off-hours. The pollen allergies of a young electrician. A tendency toward nervous soliloquy. A flair for bargain shopping. A fondness for the thousands of temporary hemispheres that bubbles of sea foam leave in the sand. An almost preadolescent slightness of frame: stringy arms and legs on a torso as slim as a grasshopper's. Softheartedness. Ambidextrousness. Irritability. He is one among countless ghosts, he finally understands, all of them a miscellany of fragments, though how those fragments have made him precisely the spirit he is he will never understand: a ghost of frugal habits and impeccable hygiene, a lover of cats, bow ties, and the smell of chlorine, in the great mix-and-match game of the universe.

FIFTY-NINE

A LESSER FEELING

It is his lot in life to be not a person but a feeling, and one of the lesser feelings at that: not love, or malice, or lust or rage or delight, but indifference. He is not the only such lesser feeling in the world. Far from it. In his neighborhood alone live four others, each of them, like him, a particular variety of indifference. There is the lukewarm resignation who runs the TV repair shop; the cool disinterest he met once at a dinner party; the numbness toward the pleasures of life whose path he sometimes crosses at the drugstore; and the gray-weather listlessness—an ideal neighbor in his way—who occupies the apartment downstairs from him. All of them exist as the individuation of a particular mood, occupying a distinct coordinate within the sphere of some larger sentiment, one specific member of an expansive heredity of emotions, yet a unique member, unduplicated, filling a single affective point to its very furthest distensions. Even the most glorious feeling, the shade of indifference tries to remind himself, cannot stretch beyond its own boundaries. All of them have their limits. Which is to say that any love he might come across is only a *kind* of love, any awe only a *kind* of awe. For all he knows they feel just as tiny as he does. He himself belongs only broadly speaking to the family of indifference. More narrowly he is what one might call a half-hearted apathy; more narrowly still a bothersomely juvenile unconcern; and more narrowly than that a barely disguised obliviousness of the type that children between the ages of seven and nine display when failing to pay attention to what might one day turn out to be crucial lifesaving information. As long as someone, anyone, remains capable of experiencing such an emotion, he—that emotion—will continue to exist. Being such a lesser feeling, ordained to so long a life, has compelled him to a certain humility. He is aware that, in the eyes of the world, he is not terribly important. He often wishes that he had been fated to a more profound existence. He envies the feelings of kings and lovers, of heroes, the feelings exalted in story and song. If only, he commonly thinks, his own blood ran with that sort of passion. But while all of this is true, he is aware how much luckier he is than some. Take those others, the ones he sees every day, who are not feelings at all but people. They rush here and there, pouring themselves through one emotion after another, like dirt through a row of sieves. Their lives pass so quickly they might as well be ghosts. From any but the most sidelong angle they seem not to be there at all.

GHOSTS

✦ AND ✦

BELIEF

SIXTY

A SMALL DISRUPTION OF REALITY

Whether the afterlife was located overhead, as the Aborigines believed, or underground, as the Greeks and the Mesopotamians contended, was answered definitely last September when, with a sound like a brush fire, the membrane between this world and the next ruptured and it became evident that death was situated, as the Narragansett had always maintained, to the southwest. Not, it should be understood, to the southwest of any particular point, but to the southwest of *every* particular point: the brick courtyard next to the Hostel Budva, the grassy bend in the Stanley Esplanade, the beach behind the Chatham Pier Fish Market, the stone steps of the Plaza Baquedano. The afterlife's appearance was simultaneous, omnifarious, and continuous. Wherever you happened to be, on that late-September day with the sun's rays blanketing the earth, or on that late-September night with an almond sliver of moon in the sky, a rift opened up just a yard or two away from you, at an azimuth of exactly 225 degrees.

What lay behind the rift was difficult to say: some shifting allness of color and motion over which the eyes seemed to skip like a stone. It might have been white but might just as plausibly have been black, or gray, or transparent. The edges were friendlier to investigation than the center was. From the evidence of the trees, clouds, and buildings against which the opening appeared like a gash, it was roughly as tall as a bus shelter and roughly as broad as a wine cask. Its borders were not static but pulsed and fluttered. And through it came pouring a great wind of ghosts. This wind of ghosts was neither hot nor cold. It blew powerfully, even aggressively, but failed to discompose so much as a single blade of grass. To the senses it offered little more than a distant smell of dust and ammonia, plus a faint ionic zizz that resembled the vibration of a dying lightbulb. Yet turning to face it, you had to catch your breath. Call it limbo or call it paradise, it was only a few steps away.

Since that day, the ghosts have never stopped blowing. Occasionally now, in a fit of morbid ebullience, what the Germans call *Todbegeisterung,* someone will brave the wind to cross the barrier between this world and the next. Whether sick or healthy, young or old, these travelers all wear the same expression: an elsewhere look of zealous distraction. To someone standing nearby—a spouse or a child, a friend or a stranger— they might say "Goodbye" or "Excuse me." Usually, though, they will leave without so much as a word, turning their feet abruptly to the southwest and pegging upstream until they vanish into the afterlife, that strange disburdening of lights and shapes that is either as much of nothing as anyone has ever seen or so much of everything that it merely looks like nothing.

SIXTY-ONE

THE ABNORMALIST AND THE USUALIST

The two senior faculty members at the Center for the Study of Theoretical Scripture were not colleagues so much as adversaries. Both of them specialized in the New Testament canon, specifically the Synoptic Gospels, but the older of them had made his reputation as a Usualist, while the younger was rapidly gaining fame as an Abnormalist. The Usualist, a near-sighted gentleman with a knack for menacing appearances, contended that all things supernatural were bunkum. As such, he had devoted his career to ridding the Scriptures of their miracles and wonders, their exorcisms, resurrections, and transfigurations, each and every hint of the hereafter or the divine. Such appeals to the otherworldly were, he maintained, relics of a simpler and more credulous age, and therefore had to go. The Abnormalist, a red-faced fellow with the habit of swinging around corners as though his fingers were the hinge and his body the door, insisted that the very *purpose* of Scripture was to reveal the numinous within the everyday. He had made it his mission, therefore, to purge the Gospels of all their laws, genealogies, and denunciations, together with their baptisms and benedictions, their dusty roadside lectures, their ordinary suppers. It was not the commonplace he intended to repudiate, he often quipped, but the *merely* commonplace, the humdrum. Both of the senior faculty members at the Center for the Study of Theoretical Scripture sifted through the Gospels fastidiously, verse by verse, the one panning for the gold of the demonstrable, the other for the gold of the ineffable. To the Abnormalist, the Usualist's scholarship was just so much wallpaper and weeds. To the Usualist, the Abnormalist's was all ghostliness and puffery. Each of them had proclaimed as much, publicly, many times. These days, when they met each other in the corridors of the Center for the Study of Theoretical Scripture, they no longer bothered to exchange hellos, yet one afternoon, as was bound to happen, the Usualist strode squinting into the copy room just as the Abnormalist came pivoting out. The two of them collided, keeling over in an eruption of books and papers. "Must this office always be your personal playground?" the Usualist snapped. "Why can't you keep your eyes open?" the Abnormalist rejoined. From his fiberglass chair in the hallway, the Center's lone adjunct faculty member, a Parablist, who held that even the plainest fact was a story that proposed some alternate meaning, watched the two of them shouting and tangling their limbs together as they attempted to stand up. Inwardly he grinned, reflecting how, despite the inexhaustible quarrels of matter and spirit, life was harmonious and sweet, and the world something magnificent.

SIXTY-TWO

REAL ESTATE

If you'll join me up here, ma'am, you'll see that the rafters are lit from below by antique sanctuary lamps. This gives the shadows what we call a "thicketing" quality, perfect for eerie half-sightings or spider-like plunges. Down here along the south wall we have the confessional. The curtains are made of opaque cotton velvet. They reach all the way to the floor, you'll notice. Now what does that mean? I'll tell you what it means. It means that, without whisking them open, no one can determine whether or not the booth is occupied, or by what. It could hold an innocent old lady, or a schoolboy, or a body with the flesh of its hands peeled all the way back to the wrists, its face frozen in a pallor of ghastly fear. Or it might be empty. Or just *seem* empty. Regardless, if you're human and you want to find out, you have to part those curtains. Over here to the right is the votive rack. At this time of night it's not in use, of course, but believe me, come seven or eight a.m., it will be quivering with candle flames. Dozens of them. Imagine the parishioners *igniting* as they say their prayers. You can practically hear it, can't you? First the whoosh, then the squeal, then an inferno of arms and legs drawing air. Now the altar in back of the chancel is original to the space. It dates to the 1840s, as do the chalice and cross. I know what you're thinking, but let me tell you, ma'am, they might seem innocuous, but pervade a holy object like that—not just haunt it, but *saturate* it—and it will become positively menacing. Nothing is more disquieting to worshippers than wine that turns to curds in the mouth. I know from experience. Ah, I see the stained-glass window has caught your attention. You're right to admire it. Notice how the Virgin and Child seem to smile down on the church with an exalted benevolence, as if to say, One day all your pains will be comforted, one day all your happiness restored. But look: with just the subtlest contortion of the lead—there, where the Child's eyes meet His brow—His face takes on an aura of predatory menace. And see: the Virgin is still smiling, yes, but smiling the way a slave smiles to placate Her master. And of course, as I know you're well aware, it doesn't take much to turn a window into a cataract of glass. To the left here is the baptismal font. Mind you don't touch the water. Now if you'll follow me through this door, ma'am, I can show you the sacristy. It was in this room, shortly before last month's unfortunate exorcism, that the priest was found strangled by his vestments. The new fellow they've brought in is just a pup, still convinced of Creation's essential goodness. "A blind panic opportunity," as we in the business call them. Out back is the graveyard, but then I don't need to tell *you* that, do I? I should make it clear, ma'am, this place is going to go fast. It has every modern amenity—amenities by the thousands. 15,617 of them, in fact, according to the parish's latest roster. All that's missing is a tenant. If you're interested, you should let me know as soon as possible. Tonight. Yes, ma'am. We can move you in right away.

SIXTY-THREE

WHICH ARE THE CRYSTALS,
WHICH THE SOLUTION

That man in the corduroy jacket, waiting in his car for the traffic light to change, is not a pessimist but a fatalist. He believes people can generally expect things to turn out for the best but that he, in particular, is doomed. He is not wrong. Some years ago, unbeknownst to him, he attracted the notice of a "teasing spirit," mischievous if not downright hostile, what his Polish grandfather used to call a *psotnik*. What the man did to provoke the spirit, she—the spirit—can no longer recollect, but ever since he did it, she has served out an array of punishments, inducing his life toward dishevelment, inconvenience, and humiliation. Her specialty is love. The voice that keeps whispering to him—whispering tenderly, persistently— that his most necessary happiness is hiding behind the face of some woman he barely knows and whose inner life he can only dimly imagine is hers: the spirit's. Her most recent selection is the receptionist at the library, ten years the man's junior. The woman's slender fingers play over her keyboard like water trickling through a rickrack of stones, and the man has found that he can't stop picturing them disarranging his hair. Even better, from the spirit's perspective, is that *she* seems as nervous in *his* presence as *he* does in *hers*, exactly the kind of blundering the man is inclined to mistake for attraction. *Make*

another excuse to drop by and talk to her, the spirit prods. *Ask her to dinner,* the spirit suggests. *It won't be awkward,* the spirit insists. *Do it.* Gleefully she anticipates the look that will wash through the woman's eyes, and then immediately through the man's, when it becomes plain that, by asking her out, he is obligating her to reject him, and that, by obligating her to reject him, *he* has wounded *her,* leaving her no choice but to parry the jab, no matter how kind she might wish to be. It is all so delicious. But the man is stopped right now at the corner of Evergreen and Mississippi, alone in his car, and the spirit will have to save that trap for later. Instead, with an ability born of her spite, occult and unappeasable, she pierces the signal box at the base of the traffic post and stems the electricity in a particular loop of wire. The man in the corduroy jacket sees the side lights switch from green to yellow. He eases his foot off his brake, allowing his car to bump slightly forward, but though the opposing lane receives a long through-signal, his own light remains stubbornly red. He replaces his foot on the brake. Why do so many four-way lights fail to complete their cycles? he wonders. Invariably the first three operate exactly as they should, but the fourth light, his light, always malfunctions. Before long, to his left and right, cars are accelerating back into the intersection. Of course, he thinks. Here it is again. The endless red light, training itself toward him like the needle of a compass.

SIXTY-FOUR

COUNTLESS STRANGE
COUPLINGS AND SEPARATIONS

They made him leave the afterworld when they found out he was not a ghost. Asked directly, he was forced to confess the truth—that he was living and breathing—and before he knew it he was back on earth, sitting on a thermoplastic steel bench in the food court of a shopping mall. Atoms were pinballing every which way. Mobs of people were galumphing around inside their fat and muscle. His stomach ached from what he gradually identified as hunger. Oh, great, he thought. *This* again. To his left was a noodle bar, to his right a fried chicken counter, but the thought of taking the matter he possessed and adding yet more matter to it repulsed him. He was practically bursting with the stuff already. He had to admit he found the haste with which he had been banished from the afterworld galling. What, after all, was his real offense? "Willful and premeditated materiality": that, word for word, was the accusation they had leveled against him. As for "materiality"—well, okay, he couldn't deny the charge. But "willful"? "Premeditated"? A more deplorable mischaracterization of his motives he could hardly imagine. If you asked him, his expulsion was unjust, and not only unjust but profoundly so, elementally so. The fact that he had not yet died, while true, was a mere technicality. Surely they would have realized as much if they had allowed him to argue his case. Not that he didn't understand their concerns. No one wanted to find the gates between life and death demolished, the otherworld teeming with lookie-loos, tourists, and honeymooners. But he was no tourist, no lookie-loo, didn't they see? He was one of *them:* pensive, ceremonious, a ghost in all but essence. He had never been at ease with himself—not, at least, as a corporeal being. Five minutes back in the world and already he felt just like everyone else, a big bag of skin sloshing with water and proteins. Through his clothing he could feel the empty diamonds of the bench against his thighs. Wherever he looked, another piece of matter was moving, changing, decaying, or maturing. Light was agglutinating on every available surface. No, no, no. It just wouldn't do. He intended to file the paperwork to contest his deportation as soon as possible—or, barring that, to die, and to die just as quickly as he could arrange it. One way or another he was determined to return to the afterlife, his proper home, where everything slid pleasantly toward nonbeing. And with that thought, he stood up and strode to the mall's glass doors. Outside he was sure he would find what he needed—either an attorney with a specialty in the transcendental or a good, heavy, fast-moving car.

SIXTY-FIVE

RAPTURE

✝

Mostly it happened just like the Scriptures said it would. The plains swallowed the mountains, the waters turned to blood, disease and warfare thundered across the continents, and whatever paradise the future might once have promised lay in an appalling wreckage of masonry, char, and bones, but then the trumpets sounded, and the skies rolled open, and five billion faces were lifted, like sunflowers, to the brightness of His coming. No prophecy could have reproduced the beauty of that light; after so long, and in the gravest of hours, Jesus. Believers the world over dropped to their knees. That they had misunderstood His story, and in what way, they did not yet suspect. The introductory sign came shortly after He descended from the firmament to prepare the earth for the dawn of His kingdom, though almost no one recognized it. As He began to walk among them, an old woman, palsied along her left side, reached for the hem of His garment. Her hand swept through it intangibly, clapping against the pavement. Asked on camera what His robe had felt like, she answered in a tone of puzzlement, "Like nothing. Like when I was a girl and I visited my grandfather in his barbershop and he let me play with the combs after he toweled them clean. It felt like that. Like the static charge on a hard rubber comb." Though her voice was weak, it seized everyone who heard her, not only in Jerusalem but across the world, on a billion phones and television screens. For the first time since God had scattered the races, the languages had all become one—a bygone tongue, honeyed and pure, in which each word praised His name. Soon, from the Mount of Olives, Jesus marshaled the faithful to His side. The carnage of two thousand years had made every field a battlefield, every hillside a cemetery, and when He called the departed to rise, the soil seethed with their spirits. Then, in the blinking of an eye, the living vanished from their bones and joined them. Father greeted son, and husband, wife; friend, friend, and sister, brother; yet to each other they were like a fog. Extending their arms, they found only air. From the slope of the Mount, Jesus addressed their confusion. You have died, He said, as I have died. You are shadows as I am a shadow, you are ghosts as I am a ghost. Your bodies are gone and shall not return. Truly, He said, you have all been changed. And truly they had. They were imperishable the way a draft from a cave is imperishable, imperishable the way an apparition is imperishable, imperishable because it is not alive. Of course. At last they understood. The Second Coming had finally taken place. It was the Resurrection that never had.

SIXTY-SIX

666

After ages of bartering and seduction, the Devil had accumulated the souls of so many sinners that they were like pennies to him. He spent them by the thousands just to get rid of them. Two thousand souls for a porcelain serving bowl. Three thousand for a set of neoprene hand weights. Ten thousand five for a boar-bristle hairbrush. No matter how extortionate the price, or how chintzy the merchandise, he paid up without a second thought, declining to haggle even when he knew it would be perceived as an insult. What were they to him, these divine sparks, these eternal spirits? If he dropped a few while fishing for change, what difference did it make? In fact, with each soul he squandered, Hell became a little more agreeable. Sinner by sinner the difference might be inappreciable, but over time, the Devil noticed, his wastefulness was having an effect. The seas of fire were no longer so choked with the damned and, as a result, the miasma of yellowish smoke that assaulted his lungs was gradually thinning out. The chorus of screams that filled the air had turned more euphonious and less chaotic, the wails of the individual sinners slightly more distinct. Inside the roar of their sextillion voices the Devil could almost hear the bright song of pain they used to sing. He remembered the jubilation with which he had welcomed his first lost soul—that scrawny wet-eyed woman hobbling through the cavern in her wretchedness and confusion—and the feeling, as he watched her test her steps out on the coals, that in all his trials and misfortunes there had perhaps been some furtive meaning, since through them he had come into this, his inheritance. Now that soul was indistinguishable from all the others, no more precious or golden than a swarm of mites in a blotch of sunlight. Weeds, he thought. Pennies. He wasted a hundred thousand of them on a brushed-nickel hand blender, a million five on a waterbed with a walnut frame, a few million more on a three-piece sectional sofa with a tufted ottoman. Still his coffer of souls was bursting. Finally he hired the priciest architectural firm he could find, met with its top designers and engineers, and instructed them to build him a mansion with many rooms, large enough to hold his countless useless possessions. Spare no expense, he ordered, and indeed they did not, leaving the Devil cheerfully destitute. At night now he likes to sit on his veranda, reclining in his wicker love seat. Only a single sinner remains from the vast collection of souls he labored to accumulate. He listens to the fellow's pleas for mercy; amid the crackling of the flames a kind of bird-song. He has his health, he has his privacy, and he has a quiet home away from the radiance of Creation. This, he has come to believe, was all he ever wanted in the first place.

GHOSTS

✦ AND ✦

LOVE AND FRIENDSHIP

SIXTY-SEVEN

LOST AND FOUND

The boy, eleven years old and growth-spurt thin, and wearing a hand-me-down jersey spattered with peroxide stains, was riding his bicycle around the block when his ghost deserted him. A giant white jellybean of a thing, it corkscrewed over the bike's handlebars, vaulted into the air, and took a plunge through the wire basket where he carried his chips, gloves, and thermos. He had just enough time to think, *Hey, that's mine,* before the ghost veered like a bird toward the side of the road. Quickly, before it could disappear into the Hennens' manicured boxwoods, he snatched hold of it. At home he attempted to return the ghost to his body, but no matter what strategy he employed, it would not stay put. He stuffed it under his shirt, for instance, cradling its bulge in his hands. Within seconds, though, it had broken free, slithering out from beneath the hem. He gave it a second try, making a little prison cell for the ghost by tucking his shirt into his jeans. This time it escaped through one of his sleeves. He experimented with twine, glue, rubber cement, Scotch tape, Band-Aids, gauze, and carpenters' putty. Nothing worked. He was going about this all wrong, he decided. How—from what opening—had the ghost escaped from inside him to begin with? That was the question. If his body possessed a secret hatchway, it would probably be somewhere in his chest, he reckoned, though he wasn't sure why he thought so. It just made sense to him. So he climbed onto his bed, gripped the ghost in a wrestler's X, and let himself plunge to the floor, hoping to powerslam it back through his skin. Instead, as usual, it went gassing off into the room. The boy was stumped. He had to admit it. The idea came to him to try swallowing the ghost, but while he managed to jam it into his mouth, he felt like he was working to eat a balloon, one that would not pop. It bulged against his cheeks and made his tongue taste the way spray paint smells. Finally, a few hours after the ghost had abandoned his body, the boy carried it into his front yard. He felt that he had no choice but to let it go. Immediately it fled toward the oak trees at the end of the block. He lost sight of it in the maze of their branches. With a sting of disappointment—the kind, at eleven, he was already learning to expect from life—he went back inside. The next morning, though, to his surprise, he opened his curtains to see the ghost swirling around the basketball post in his driveway. And late that afternoon, at the pool, he saw it hiding beneath the deck of the diving board. And that evening, when his parents took him out for hamburgers, he saw it pillowed in the recess of the towering yellow McDonald's M. From that day forward, the ghost maintained a bashful independence, often nearby but never actually within his reach. It was like a stray animal who, though it might approach the boy with affection, would bolt immediately from his touch; not quite his, he felt, but his enough.

SIXTY-EIGHT

ANOTHER MAN IN A MIRROR

Eventually he recognized the truth: the reason his face no longer seemed to belong to him and he had taken like a cat to avoiding his gaze in mirrors, puddles, laptop screens, and display cases was that he was, if only metaphorically, a ghost. Months or years, maybe even decades ago, there had come some fleeting second when he wasn't paying attention and he had died, but by then his habits had grown so instinctive that he simply carried on without realizing it, imitating the life he had long ago devised for himself. The more he thought about it, the more sense it made. Why else would keys, pens, and remote controls slip so regularly through his fingers? Why else would his days seem so unreal? When was the last time he had felt his emotions combusting inside him the way they did when he was fifteen, sitting alive in a darkened movie theater with his girlfriend's hand on his thigh, so exotically aware of himself that afterward, when the two of them walked into the brightness of the afternoon, he was obliged to pretend that what left him staggering for balance was in fact the sunlight? When, for that matter, was the last time he had shut down the computer or turned off the TV at night knowing that the past fourteen or sixteen hours had actually demanded his participation? He had heard it said that even more intangible than the physical world to ghosts were their own inner natures. Gone along with their bodies were their desire, their vehemence, their misery, their glee. As such, they were never outraged or anguished by their condition, just mildly self-pitying. They understood what they were missing, but only dimly, as if death were a matter of negligence, some box on a form they had failed to check. All of this described him perfectly. And so, resigned to his circumstances, he filled his hours pretending to live in a body that was pretending to grow older. He shaved his stubble that was pretending to gray and kneaded his shoulders that were pretending to ache. He pretended to wake and pretended to sleep, pretended to eat and pretended to drink, and every so often he found a woman who failed to see him for who he was—or who was, herself, a ghost—and pretended to have sex with her, all the while waiting for the years to catch up with him so that he could stop pretending. Once, though, following an hour in the dark with such a woman, he was courageous enough to meet his own eyes in the mirror. His face, to his astonishment, no longer seemed like a ghost's, like a mask from which all the selfhood had been removed. For those few seconds, he could have sworn he was real again. If only he could spend the next thirty or forty years making love, he thought, or having just finished making it, he might remain that way: alive.

SIXTY-NINE

THE APOSTROPHES

A ruinously shy bachelor had just mopped up after himself and was snapping his boxers back into place when, out of the corner of his eye, he saw something swaying through the air like a dandelion seed. He turned to take a closer look. Suspended approximately three feet to his left, at roughly the height of the light switch, was the ghost of his latest ejaculation. It was small and meek, a mere apostrophe of a thing. Nonetheless, he felt that its presence constituted an offense, maybe even a deliberate mockery. He had, after all, finished with it. For it to float there, bobbing so nonchalantly about, seemed graceless, impertinent. Rude, he thought, and he said it out loud: "Rude." The ruinously shy bachelor had been raised a Catholic, and he could not help but wonder if the apostrophe was a message from God, a curse, rebuking him for all the times he had given in to temptation and vacated himself into a Kleenex. He stepped forward, thinking either to grab the apostrophe or to swat it to the floor. With a tilting weightlessness, though, it sailed out of his reach. He feinted toward the radiator, then lunged at it again. Once more it eluded him. The nerve! All right, fine then, he thought, and adamantly, speaking as if to a pet, said, "You stay right there." When he went to the bathroom to wash his hands, though, the apostrophe followed or rather escorted him, maintaining its customary three-foot distance, as if strung to him by an invisible wire. What might have seemed a polite gap in other circumstances was plainly, in these, a taunt. Moreover, now that he had addressed the apostrophe directly, it was, for some reason, chirping. The noise resonated against the porcelain tiles—an awful tuneless burlesque. Just imagine what it would be like to go to work in such a state, thought the ruinously shy bachelor. The embarrassment would practically obliterate him. He was standing at the sink when he had an idea. He pivoted, turning his left side to the shower stall so that the apostrophe orbited swiftly onto the shampoo rack. Then he shut the curtain and bolted from the bathroom, slamming the door behind him. There. He gave a proud bark of a laugh. No muss, no fuss. But when he rested his back against the wall, he found that the apostrophe was once again beside him, hovering the same three feet to his left. By certain measures, he supposed, he should call himself lucky. Think of the countless other ghosts he might have created over the years, ghosts he could quite easily, by the friction of his hand, have coaxed into being, but which, by the grace of God, he had not. The shame the idea provoked in him was powerful, and maybe that was all it took, for all at once, to every side, in a chorus of sound, thousands of apostrophes began activating themselves like crickets.

SEVENTY

A MAN IN A MIRROR

That woman in the owl-eye glasses leads a life of secrecy and ritual. In the morning before she leaves for work, and in the evening before she goes to sleep, she always spends two hours staring into the mirror by her front door: four hours total, each and every day, without fail. For years this has been her habit, though not, as you might suspect, because she loves her own reflection. Her nose roosts too low on her face, for one thing. Her chin is too broad and bony. And her freckles, once her best feature, have gone gray along with her hair. No, when she addresses the mirror, she does so at an angle, gazing not *at* herself but *past* herself. Some years ago, on her way out the door, she was adjusting the pendant on her necklace when a sudden glassiness of motion caught her eye. At first she mistook it for a flaw in the mirror's silver. Then the flaw startled her by roping its arms over its head and opening its mouth in a helpless yawn, so recognizably human and yet so obviously immaterial that she knew at once that it—that *he*—was a ghost.

Every day since then, as if by appointment, she has watched the ghost's comings and goings. Only in the small Venetian mirror by the front door does she see him, and even then only occasionally, when his activities happen to intersect with the living room, the hallway, or the outermost edge of her kitchen. Now and then he behaves with what seems to be affection toward what seem to be people, knitting his fingers around as if tying a ribbon in someone's hair, for instance, or rocking back and forth as if embracing someone from behind. From this she has judged that he has a wife and daughter, though they have never, as he has, taken shape in the silver. Once, nearly a decade ago, upon a rainy April eight a.m., he approached the mirror to inspect his teeth. He was channeling a fingernail between his incisors when he accidentally met her eyes. For a few seconds, as his face did something curious, her knees locked and her toes began to tingle. Her heart seemed to beat at the same lazy pace as the world. She realized she was in love. Ever since then, she has been waiting for it to happen again.

On the first Saturday of each month, the woman in the owl-eye glasses puts on her best silk blouse and her pressed denim skirt and heads out for lunch with her friend the manicurist, who works in a little shop across the street. Last week, over burgers and fries, she almost told her about the ghost. Instead, though, she confessed a different secret altogether: how she fantasizes, and often, about erasing the past fifty years of her life and starting over again, awakening as she used to be, a skinny girl with red hair and freckles, whose decisions had not yet been made, whose rituals had not yet been established, and who could never imagine that fifty years later, in her loneliness and disappointment, she would long to trade her life away. "Are you," her friend asked in a voice of almost unbearable sympathy, "seeing someone?"

SEVENTY-ONE

TURNSTILES

In the house at the top of the cul-de-sac live a fickle couple in their mid-forties: she a vacillating woman with a watercolory pink complexion, he a temperamental man with a broom-bristle haircut. The two of them are sometimes happily, sometimes miserably, but on the whole rather volatilely married. At the heart of their relationship is the problem of inconstancy—a changeability so profound that it does not seem improper to call it spiritual. Both the husband and the wife flit from job to job and hobby to hobby. Both display the most extreme vicissitudes of taste and style. And neither of them can ever be sure, from one instant to the next, whether their natures will impel them toward insecurity or self-confidence, pensiveness or conviviality, tidiness or dishevelment. Some mornings they wake up inexplicably despising each other, others just as inexplicably idolizing each other, and if occasionally, in their daily gyrations, they achieve a propitious moment of understanding, no sooner does it happen than one or the other of them will perform an about-face and they will become strangers again. The only real personal continuity either of them has ever experienced is material, corporeal, physiognomic. That pink face: to him, it is his wife. And that shock of yellow hair: it is her husband. To the two of them, the saying "You are who you are" has the quality not of a truism but of a koan. Their predicament, though they do not realize it, is that inside each of them, where their souls should be, is an empty room with a clattering turnstile. They are not individuals but way stations. Every day thousands of departing spirits pass through them on their journey between life and death. The spinning that both of them think of as their personhood, that swerving quality of the heart, is just the coming and going of those spirits: old men and women who can't believe how swiftly the years have spiraled away, car crash victims spruced up for the prom or the nightclub, battered children clutching silk blankets and teddy bears, cancer patients with scarves where their hairlines should be. If she, the vacillating woman, has always felt a deep inner restlessness, and if he, the temperamental man, often fails to recognize himself, how could it be otherwise? For the two of them, in lieu of enduring souls, there has been only a lifetime of other people's ghosts, along with a faint awareness of how violable it is to be a human being, and how difficult to remain just one.

SEVENTY-TWO

A TRUE STORY

He was in love with her and, for that reason, wanted to end it. She was in love with him and, in spite of it, wanted to stay together. They spent the last evening of their holiday in the heat and stillness of the hotel room, she on the sofa, he on the wing chair, trying to decide whether what they felt for each other was impossible to resist or impossible to bear; a consolation, as she thought, or a punishment, as he did. Every so often they leaned forward to mouse at each other's faces with their noses. Crowd noises floated up from the avenue beside the Arno—laughter, and then a saxophone. Finally, exhausted, they queued up a relaxation video on her laptop and, in the enfolding static of a prerecorded rain shower, went to bed. He was not prone to hallucinations, and did not believe in ghosts, but deep in the night he came awake and saw her apparition. She was striding toward the window that opened out onto the spalletta and the river, dressed in a black kimono with a pattern of white vines and small flexed leaves on the fabric, a garment he knew without question was hers, even though he had never seen it before. The loose skirt was jelly-fishing around her waist, flourishing slowly in and out, which made it look like she was swimming. At first he presumed she had waited for him to fall asleep before she got up, as she so often did, to pace the room. He could hear her feet brushing the hardwood with a *swish-swish-swish,* like the wind making patterns out of the rain. Then he reached for her side of the bed, felt the top of her hand, and saw that she was still lying there. The woman in the kimono was *not* her then. Or at least not her body. She was something else—something drained, heedless; not her but something that wore the costume of her. He might have been frightened, but no, he realized: he too was something else. A child could have named the feeling. It was still there the next morning as they locked their door with the cumbersome iron key and rolled their luggage to the curb. And there on the plane as they watched the terrible in-flight movie. And there twelve hours later, on the other side of the Atlantic, as she pressed her palm to his stomach and said, with what he wished he could hear as incredulity, "You didn't change your mind." They examined each other's faces, tenderly but as if from a great distance. What, it occurred to him, if the ghost had not been hers but *his:* a specter who had manifested itself to usher him out of his life? What if this airport terminal with the customs agent repeating "Exits are to the left, connecting flights are to the right" was only a death-dream? What if his heart had given out in the bed of that old Italian hotel? Well then, he thought. So much the better. Years from now she could tell herself that he had never left her, not for good, that there had still been time for him to change his mind. How his faith in her had weakened but not beyond repair. How his heart had loved her and then it stopped.

SEVENTY-THREE

BULLETS AND WHAT IT TAKES TO DODGE THEM

That August, when they called it quits, her friends told her that she had dodged a bullet, and his told him that he had. The truth, at least initially, was that he was convinced the fault was his—certain that he had ignored her distresses and sensitivities, expressed so clearly and so often, and thereby blundered into breaking her heart—while she, for her part, was remorseful for taking such quick offense at every careless thing he said, and equally convinced the fault was hers. Before long, though, with the encouragement of their friends, they were each won around to the version of the story that most effectively consoled and exonerated them. He said to himself, If she wasn't capable of trusting me, she wasn't capable of trusting anyone. And in return she said, He confessed right away to his minor shortcomings but was totally blind to his actual faults.

Their love affair had ended abruptly, after once again, to her incredulity, he had suggested that her parents, so hidebound and dictatorial, were surely more loving than she was capable of realizing, while it became apparent to him that all this time, privately, beneath the theater of her smiles, she had been livid over his slights and discourtesies, slights and discourtesies he was astonished to discover she had ever attributed to him at all but that had reduced her, she said, many times, to tears.

What he had regarded as evenhandedness she had regarded as callousness, what she had regarded as vulnerability he had regarded as violence, and since there was no impartial jury to whom they could appeal for a verdict, each of them continued to believe, when they considered their spell of sexual intoxication, that only one of them was the wrongdoer, only one the wrongdone.

Something about the suddenness with which the relationship had ended kept its memory fresh in their minds. In stray moments, they would each find themselves annotating and revisiting it—first in the weeks and months that followed, then as they grew older and the years went by, and finally after they died and the years no longer did. As ghosts, they discovered, they still occupied the precise contours of their own lives, but less fleetly than they had before, more lingeringly. Death was a kind of forever, but one that pervaded the past rather than transcended it. Bodies moved through time as quickly as fire. Ghosts moved through time as slowly as glass. As such, there was plenty of opportunity for the two of them to watch the people they once had been, a man and a woman like all men and women, whistling so fast through their days, so fast; hurtling into other bodies sometimes, and sometimes barely missing them. From the perspective of the dead, life was a dangerous thing: a world of bullets, with everyone dodging everyone else, and no one to blame but God or the cosmos, contingency or fate, whoever had fired the gun.

SEVENTY-FOUR

KNEES

A bachelor and an introvert, with a monotonous data-entry job and a wait-and-see attitude toward life, is perusing the morning's paper when he discovers, with less surprise than he might have, his first girlfriend's obituary. *Complications following. Survived by. Age forty-seven.* Once, long ago, in their morbid adolescence, all white Pan-Cake makeup and black eyeliner, she had asked him, "If you could pick someone's ghost to haunt you, whose would it be?" and he had answered, "Yours. No question." They were smoking cigarettes at the bare-dirt back corner of the high school. "*Really?*" she had quizzed him. "What if I was, like, a *pissed-off* ghost?" She was pissed off all the time anyway, ghost or no ghost, and he told her so. She frog-punched him. "Ow!" he said. "I mean, you're halfway there already. Ow! Ow! Hey, wait, I *love* you pissed off," and you know what? He meant it. She had the kind of temper that advertised itself in frowns and edicts and bizarre discharges of static electricity, which she was able to deploy on purpose, the way other people deployed curse words. Doggedness was how he thought of it. Doggedness regarding the music she liked and the music she hated; regarding clothing, grammar, politics— everything; and the same doggedness when it came to him: his lips, and his fingertips, and the rodlike tendons in his neck. He had never believed anyone would find him attractive, or funny. He couldn't resist her. "Let's say you're middle-aged and boring one day," she continued, "and I've died, okay? You're wearing a blue button-up shirt with short sleeves, because you've lost your fashion sense, and you're drinking coffee with too much milk, because you've lost your taste buds. Suddenly you see a fly drowning in the coffee. Picture its wings, its black legs. Two seconds ago it wasn't there. You have this image of it bobbing up from the bottom of the mug, like an air bubble, but no—it must have fallen mid-flight." Now, so many years later, on an uncommonly cold summer morning, he is sitting at the Formica-and-aluminum table he inherited after his parents died. In his coffee, as yellow as old ivory, is a housefly, its little black prayer legs making bubbles in the liquid. "That whisper tickling your ear: you could swear it's me. But when you turn around, I'm not there. It's high summer—July—but there's a chill in the air." All at once he feels a jabbing sensation, as if someone has frog-punched him. "Pop! A knuckle mark rises in the crook of your arm. Then you hear something shuffling around beneath the kitchen table. Knees. You're really saying you love me enough, even all dead and pissed off like I am, that you would bend down hoping to see me?" she asked. And he answered, "You bet your life." The kiss she gave him tasted like Starbursts and tobacco. Even now, as something steals toward him beneath the table, he remembers the flavor of it. Through his khakis he feels a nip of static electricity. He flinches. And looks. And loves and is afraid of her.

SEVENTY-FIVE

THE MAN SHE IS TRYING TO FORGET

That woman with the long neck and the narrow shoulders is searching for a man to forget another one. She began her search nearly a year ago, at the basement bar half a block from her apartment building, before moving on to other bars in other neighborhoods, then to museums and yoga studios, political rallies and supermarkets. Each night she leaves home ceremonially, in a hush of deliberation. She feels like an acolyte proceeding toward the altar. In her skirt and her heels she steps carefully, pauses, steps again. Listens to her clothing rustle. Waits patiently by the crosswalk. The brake lights of cars flicker. Store signs tick and buzz. The city has a different cologne after the sun falls. She breathes it in. Maybe this, she thinks, will be the night she finds him, at the bar or the art gallery, the health club or the cooking class. He will fix her with a smile and a tilt of the head, then enfold her in conversation, the man whose company will outshine or obliterate the man who has broken her heart. But it never happens. Oh, she meets men, of course she does—whole casts of them, whole orchestras—but they always remind her of the man she is trying to forget, at least tenuously, and sometimes uncannily. This one has his build; this one, his posture. This one wears his expression of slightly cross-grained amusement, visible mainly across the lips and the eyes, as if he has never stopped expecting a teacher to chastise him for letting his attention wander. This man likes the same movies he does; this one, the same music. This man sneezes once, then sneezes again: two times without fail. This one has neglected to shave his Adam's apple, too prominent to be considered shapely or beautiful, yet alluring for all that, though its troughs and escarpments must be a hazard to his razor. This one shares his focused, almost gladiatorial, approach to card games and pool. This one expresses the same skepticism toward what he calls the supernatural, by which he means ghosts, angels, astrology, reincarnation—but also fate, karma, "vibes." A dozen men might buy her a drink, a dozen more might offer her their number, but the result is always the same. The effort aggravates and depletes her. She feels as if something that once quivered before her almost visibly, shining from the tips of her fingers, has been extinguished. Increasingly she suspects that the man she is trying to forget is literally, definitionally, unforgettable. It is not that his characteristics are universal. He simply has too many of them. Her only hope, she thinks, is to find a man with no characteristics at all, or else with one characteristic and one alone: the vision to see her as the woman who will overshadow the woman who once broke his heart.

SEVENTY-SIX

THE ETERNITIES

Her husband was affectionate, charming, wealthy, handsome, and considerate, and also fundamentally heartless. Imagine a tropical island that is all shore and no interior: sure, the sand might warm your toes, and the breeze might cool your skin, but try to venture inland and some mysterious turnabout will spin you around and you'll find yourself facing the waves again. That was their life together—ringed by comforts but inaccessible at the center. By the time she perceived it, she had rounded the corner into middle age. Oh, her marriage was peaceful enough, habitable enough, no question. It seemed wrong to be inundated by regrets, yet frequently, eavesdropping on herself, she would notice that she was repeating the same two words. *Somewhere* and *faraway. Faraway* and *somewhere. Somewhere, somewhere, faraway.* The distant land she was coveting was not a place at all, she realized, but a time, and that time, she understood, was not the future but the past, her own past, all those stupid happy years that had gone trembling into the air like ashes from a fire. Why couldn't she go back and try again? Surely, she thought, this was not her only life. Then she died, at fifty, of a coronary, and discovered that it was. All around her at first was a peculiar darkness, blotched and streaked with a rich red overcolor. After that came the blunted steel and the rubber gloves and a pulselessness she was almost ready to mistake for silence until she made out the buzz of an electric light. How soon she realized where she was she could not say, only that, eventually, she did. What she had been given was not a *new* life but the same life again, with the same mother and father, the same springer spaniel, the same duplex apartment with the nettles climbing the back fence. She was not a ghost exactly; or rather, if she was, she was haunting only herself, peering out at her experiences from the inside. Think of it like this: once she had been a native to her life, but this time she was a tourist, without the language to converse with anyone or the ability to affect anything. Turn left, she would command her body, and her body would turn right. Take the job overseas, she would tell herself, and her body would stay put. Marry someone else, she would say, and her body would walk the aisle, accept the ring, and offer the same old *I do*. Leave the island, she would plead. Leave the island. On her fiftieth birthday, as she was nearing the end again, she wondered if it would happen the same way this time. Would she wake up once more inside her own life, haunting not only herself but the second self who had haunted the first? How many hundreds of her might there be in here, how many thousands, standing on that slinking line where the sand soaked up the surf?

SEVENTY-SEVEN

TOO LATE

His wife was tenderhearted, idealistic, guileless, nurturing, and intuitive, but also quick to take injury from simple accidents of phrasing. He himself was simultaneously talkative and bumbling, the kind of man who said three wrong things on his way to every right one, punting figures of speech around like soccer balls. Though he tried to be gentle toward her, and she tried to be charitable toward him, it couldn't last, and didn't. His second wife was more ambitious than he was, and also more fastidious, but at twenty-six she was still a virgin. She had begun to feel as if her virginity had metastasized, like a cancer, and so, in desperation, she had married him, admitting only after their honeymoon was over that he was the wrong man. His third wife was an amateur actor and a devout Christian. She mistook his irreverence for an elaborate act of prolonged theater and was incensed when she realized how extravagantly she had misunderstood him. His fourth wife could not stop imagining all the alternate paths her life might have followed. What if she had accepted that job overseas? Kept that child? Married someone else? His fifth wife was still infatuated with her prior husband, her third, who himself, it developed, was also still infatuated with her. His sixth wife was a perfectionist, irritated not so much by *his* defects as by his failure to notice *hers.* His seventh wife was too naive for him; his eighth, too adventurous. Not until his ninth wife left him for her chiropractor was he able to diagnose his problem. He was one of love's wishful thinkers, blown this way and that by his faith in romance, and thus always vulnerable to the next woman, the next wife. He would meet someone at a lecture or a party, feel a canyony sensation of intimacy and potential, and before he knew it—bam!—another marriage. His tenth wife objected to his politics: too wishy-washy. His eleventh objected to his silences: too damning. He was preparing to wed his twelfth wife when he died. Some six months later he found himself on the other side of a Ouija board, speaking with a woman so desperate for evidence of the spirit world that her stomach kept producing sound effects, the kind of noises a bear might make, or two balloons rubbing together. "I'm sorry," she apologized, and, "Oh, dear. Forgive me." The planchette traced out his answers. F—O—R—G—I—V—E—N. "Forgiven." M—E— T—O—O. "Me, too." A—L—O—N—E. "Alone." Suddenly, by instinct, he knew that he should marry her, knew that, given the chance, this love was the one that would actually persist, but before he could ask the question, she moved the planchette to goodbye and he faded away somewhere, because in death, as in life, when it comes to questions of the heart, "You came just in time" always means "You came too late."

SEVENTY-EIGHT

DETENTION

It was a lot like school, the afterlife. That was what she discovered. Some vague time ago she had been the mousy girl with the B+'s, the one whose name the teachers struggled to recollect whenever she was missing from the head count, shy beyond all reason, and though there were no grades now, and no names, once again she felt like that girl she used to be, filing through the phases of being with the twenty-three ghosts who were her nearest contemporaries, each of whom, like her, needed some structure, a few friends, and above all else an education. There was a physics of ghostliness: *This is the force it takes to rattle the silverware. This is the energy you'll need to shake the curtains.* A social studies: *In this country you'll be seen as a harbinger of misfortune, while in that you'll be celebrated as a blessing from the ancestors.* Even an etiquette: *The west side of a room is for visitations, the east side for summonings. You should send a chill through the air before you make your appearance, never after. It's discourteous to haunt the recently bereaved unless you happen to be the ghost they are mourning.* Her weakness, then as now, was public speaking. For her to gather the confidence she needed to moan before an audience, the eloquence to skipper a planchette across a board, took considerably more courage than she possessed. She had always preferred to let her friends do the speaking for her. How typical that on the first day of her immateriality, after someone asked her how old she had been when she died and she realized, to her mortification, that she couldn't remember, another ghost with the same sheen of newness about her showed an infinitesimal twinkle of sympathy, letting a me-too smile flash across her features, and from that moment on she regarded her as her closest friend. Nothing came more naturally to her than to be the second ghost in a pair, trailing along behind the pretty one, the cheeky one. Now and then, the way a bonfire throws off a cinder, her mind would emphasize that none of this was preordained, that not only her best friend but also the boys she liked and the boys she avoided and the girl who teased her and everyone else was just an accident of the calendar, in this life just as in the last one. The randomness of it all unsettled her. So much depended upon the dates on either side of that dash: when your lungs drew air dash when your heart gave out. A few days earlier or later and fate would have scripted her existence with a different cast entirely. Occasionally, as she floated before yet another unimpressed family, attempting to produce a preternatural keen, she wondered if she would ever change. Eventually time would make her a new person, of that she was confident, if not soon then surely on her graduation day, when some other, greater death would call her name, hand her a diploma, and superintend her out of reality.

SEVENTY-NINE

I LIKE YOUR SHOES

The note read "I like your shoes." She found it spelled out in the condensation on her living room window, written glidingly, with a sort of throwaway prettiness, in strokes the width of a fingertip. When she attempted to wipe it off, her palm came back dry. Even so, it took her a moment to understand the situation. The writing was—had to be—on the *outside* of the glass. Her apartment was on the sixteenth floor, with no balconies or even window ledges. How such a message could have gotten there, who could have composed it, eluded her. The heat of the morning took hold as the sun crested the highrises, and she watched as, all at once, the words were inhaled back into the air.

The second note arrived a few months later: "I like your shoes," written in the same pleasingly rounded hand as before. She pressed her cheek to the window, searching for a suspended platform, a bungee cord, some scaffolding or suction marks, but the face of the building offered only glass and aluminum.

The third note appeared early the following winter, lingering in the frost above the kitchen sink as she washed the dishes. The familiar words—"I like your shoes"—almost escaped her notice, since the sky behind them was the same marmoreal gray as the ice.

The fourth, fifth, sixth, and seventh notes arrived on a hot April afternoon within the span of a few minutes, fading away and then replacing one another with a bellows-like breathing rhythm: "I like your shoes," "I like your shoes," "I like your shoes," "I like your shoes." By then she had moved to a third-floor walk-up in a converted school building. Her new boyfriend, obliged by his commute to wake an hour earlier than she did, often left little goodbyes for her on the kitchen counter or the dry-erase board, but his crabbed script was nothing like the declarations that had pursued her across the city, so fluidly, so puckishly made. She was certain they were not from him.

What she did not yet know, but was starting to suspect, was that the notes would accompany her for the rest of her life. That some god, ghost, or demon would go on, until the day she died, liking her shoes. And that even after eleven different houses and apartments, hundreds of guest rooms and hotel suites, seven boyfriends, two husbands, and several checkerboards' worth of windows, she would never be sure whether the message was meant to be a compliment or an insult. The phrase reminded her of the roundabout observations of teenage girls, the kind who put just enough sugar on their barbs to disguise them as flattery. Every time she went shoe-shopping, she found herself asking the same question: But what do they *really* think?

GHOSTS

✦ AND ✦

FAMILY

EIGHTY

THE GHOST'S DISGUISE

The country where he lived was full of daylight, insects, gardens, dirt, and ghosts. All his life he had heard people say, when they were ill or injured or when the ghosts grew too plentiful, "The body is the ghost's disguise," meaning, in the first case, *Remember that life is fleeting,* and in the second, *Be kind to them, for they were once like us.* But to him the creatures were a nuisance. Frequently they congregated in the aisles of his little market. When he shooed them out onto the street, saying, "What do you want with my vegetables? My stacks of dented cans? Go away now, please," they never answered him, only stared as ghosts do, with their wide, chalklike eyes. Outside, ghosts clogged the air like sedge flies, and indeed, in certain lights—at sunrise and sunset, for instance, or when the sky was yellowing after a midday shower—it was hard to distinguish the one from the other. Both of them, the ghosts and the flies, were just tall blurs of dots knitting haphazardly around inside themselves. Once, in the flexure of a certain ghost's neck, and in the way her lips seemed to brim with some mysterious smile, he thought he recognized his wife, who had died long ago following a stroke. And another time, in the modestman's hunch of a particular ghost's shoulders, he seemed to detect his favorite uncle, taken by cancer just the year before.

But both were quickly engulfed in the swirling company of apparitions. His mother used to tell him about a place called the sea, where the horizon was made of shining water and the pathways were not so crowded with spirits, but such a place, he thought, if it truly existed, lay so far away that it might as well have been the moon. To imagine that any living person had ever traveled to either one astounded him. Though he dreamed occasionally of salt waves that threw streamers of kelp across his feet, he had never ventured beyond his country's borders, feeling himself too busy when he was young and too tired now that he was old. Yet still from time to time he caught himself thinking, *Maybe someday*. All these years and still, *Maybe someday*. Amusing, the notions his brain turned out. How few were the somedays that remained to him, he thought. How many the somedays that had departed. He was not yet seventy when death murmured his name. One afternoon, sweeping the last stubborn wisp of a specter from his store, he slipped to the floor and awoke without a body. Around him was a great embracing ocean of ghosts, their pale eyes alight with curiosity and affection. Their voices were like waves that beat against the ears with a whispering sound: his wife and his uncle, his mother and father—*shish, shish, shish*. Stand up, you're here, you're awake now, they said. There was so much to do, and there was nothing to be afraid of. Death had already come and gone.

EIGHTY-ONE

A SOURCE OF CONFUSION

Some years ago, thanks to a mix-up in the order of the universe, women began giving birth to ghosts rather than babies. At first the change was bewildering, not only to the millions of sad new mothers and fathers in the world but to their doctors, their midwives, and even the ghosts themselves, if, that is, we understood what it meant when their borders wavered and their faces turned inside out. But since then, I must say, most of us have grown accustomed to the situation. The deliveries generally proceed without complication: half an hour of contractions, a sensation of deep pressure, and then, all at once, the ghost—a milky little creature that flows gracefully into the air, swaying and curling around on itself like a bubble filled with smoke before popping open and assuming its lines. Birth is still a miracle, and sometimes even a joyous one, but a miracle of a different sort, a miracle from the night side of the grave, as it were, rather than the day side. The mystery that used to envelop newborn babies—*Where does life come from?*—is mingled now with the mystery that used to envelop the dead—*Where is life going?* But I am being unnecessarily philosophical. What's important to remember is that the ghosts arrive fully mature, demanding no coddling or attention. They require no food or shelter. They are not recognizable as the people they used to be, and do not reply to the names we give them. In their multitude there are no Jims or Arthurs, no Coras or Joannas. The surest way to attract their awareness, we have found, is a pained inhalation of the kind that happens when you prick your finger with a needle, but such little gasps, though they seem to remind the ghosts of something, are only rarely successful. Once the ghosts are born, they accompany their parents home reluctantly. It is never long before they drift through the bricks and the plaster to go quietly about their business. All those grocery stores, theme parks, and old mansions where they congregate——one is tempted to use the word "haunt," but the truth is that we comprehend their motives poorly. They might be conspiring against us, or meditating, grieving or simply loitering. We have no idea. In any case, every year there are more of them and fewer of us. They don't age, or seemingly die. Or at least so far they haven't. Logic suggests that sooner or later, as we age and meet our end, this world will be theirs, though by then maybe those of us who are now alive and have since passed away will have been born little by little into their number. Somewhere, one presumes, in whatever afterlife the ghosts have deserted, stretch vast fields of babies, just as confused as we are.

EIGHTY-TWO

UNSEEABLE, UNTOUCHABLE

The game is called "Unseeable, Untouchable," or, alternatively, "Ghost." The players are the older girl, the younger girl, and the babysitter; the playing field the family room, the kitchen, and the foyer. The rules are simple: the older girl and the younger girl each must pick two of the babysitter's senses to disable—two apiece; not necessarily the same two—and the babysitter, using whichever senses remain to her, must try to catch them. For instance, the older girl, a long-necked eight-year-old with the booming voice of a theater impresario, might say, "Unseeable, unhearable!" and the younger girl, so excitable that she runs at a tilt, listing forward like a wooden top, might say, "Unseeable, unsmellable!" and then the babysitter will awaken as if from a daze, declare, "There's someone in this house with me. I'm sure of it," and pursue the girls from room to room, sniffing for the older one because she cannot see or hear her, and listening for the younger one because she cannot see or smell her. Finally, as if by luck, she will ensnare one of them, yanking at the thin bones of her arms and exulting, "I've caught one, I've caught one," until the girl changes from unseeable to untouchable and slides from the babysitter's grip. Those are the essentials of the game: not catch-me-if-you-can but catch-me-ha!-you-can't. Though the rules were originally improvised through play, they have slowly become rigid with custom. The babysitter always stumbles along with her hands frog-toed open to show that she is feeling for the girls, squints to show that she is looking for them, duck-lips at the air to show that she is tasting for them. The girls always agitate the babysitter with quick smacks to the arms and legs. Are they supposed to be living children fleeing a dead spirit, the babysitter wonders, or dead spirits taunting a living teenager? Who, in other words, is the ghost for whom the game is named? Their roles are—she recently learned the word in her English class—ambiguous. One day, as a treat for the girls, she props her phone on a windowsill and records them as they play. The video uploads itself to her profile page, where, over time, it will be engulfed by other videos, other photos, and gradually forgotten. But exactly forty-nine years later, she will tap an on-this-date notification, and there, for a minute and seven seconds, they will be: the older girl with her butterfly hair clips, the younger girl with her chubby pink cheeks, and she, the babysitter, with her chin raised for smelling, her ears cupped for hearing. By then the girls will be middle-aged. She'll do the math: fifty-two and fifty-seven. She herself will be sixty-three. Yet inside the video, which is to say back in time, which is to say now, they are all still children. Unfinished. Untested. Unready.

EIGHTY-THREE

GHOST BROTHERS

Two boys, one of them bold and one of them timid, decided to become blood brothers, but when the moment came to apply the knife to their palms, the bold one proceeded and the timid one balked. "That's all right," the bold one said. "Here. You can just pretend." With his finger he traced an imaginary blade across his friend's hand, then clasped it in his own. Between them they determined that the blood the timid one had spilled was not imaginary as such, it was supernatural— ghost blood—and, accordingly, that though the bold one was the timid one's blood brother, the timid one was the bold one's ghost brother. The difference, they decided, was this: while a blood brother's bond was immediate and lasting, inseverable for a lifetime, a ghost brother's bond, though just as strong, came with a built-in delay; it too was inseverable, but only after death. "Agreed?" the bold one asked. "Agreed," the timid one said. The two boys remained friends deep into their middle age. Through surgeries, marriages, children, and career changes, the enjoyment they took in each other never flagged, until finally, when they were both on the cusp of retirement, the timid one fell sick and died. As a ghost—and, more important, a ghost *brother*—he felt a continuing attachment to his friend. For more than fifty years, the bold one had looked out for him, making sure that he was not bullied or mistreated. Now that the baton had been handed along, the timid one resolved to do the same. From then on, within the strict limits of his disembodiment, he did his best to protect his friend—modestly, for that was his nature, but earnestly nonetheless. He moaned politely at people who cut the bold one off in line. He sent a humble chill through the air when the hospital receptionist raised her voice at him. Once, a pickpocket swooped in for the bold one's wallet at the hardware store, and the timid one sighed so disapprovingly that the fellow broke off and scuttled away down the lumber aisle. As the years stacked up, the ghost's instinct for danger sharpened to a fine edge. A day came when his friend grew dizzy collecting the mail, lifted his hands two-thirds of the way to his face, and fell to his stomach on the driveway. Death was stealing over him visibly, like smoke edging through the loose frame of a door, but the ghost shouted, "Stop that!," the ghost shouted, "Go away!," his voice so fearless that the cloud of death retreated. The bold one rose to his feet guardedly, then wiped the blood from his palms. The timid one floated unseen at his shoulder, like the ghost of a knight, the ghost of a king. He sensed that the bravery to which he had always aspired, but which he had for so long fallen short of possessing, was at last within his reach.

EIGHTY-FOUR

A SECOND TRUE STORY

A certain Russian philosopher maintained that people are not born with their souls but must labor to create them. Anyone who fails to do so, he conjectured, will dissolve upon dying into nonexistence. He was partially correct: indeed we are not born with our souls. Instead each of us is born possessing the soul of someone else, which is ours to safeguard but not to keep. Eventually, if we are lucky, our lives will introduce us to exactly the right person and the trip lever of some secret drawer will disengage, whereupon our soul will be relinquished to us—though the likelihood of an even swap (the chance, that is, that the soul we have been stewarding will belong to the same person who has been stewarding ours) is incalculably small. Take that boy, barely five years old, kneeling in his front yard beside an agreeable big wet-eyed sheepdog. He listens to her snuffling out a slow peaceful breath, then, after half a minute goes by, another. She is sweet and sad, as solemn as a cloud behind her face. Inside her body, the boy thinks, it must sound like a giant cave: a heartbeat for every breath, and a breath for every heartbeat. She is as large as he is, maybe slightly larger. It's hard to be sure, since dogs aren't shaped like people. But there's one thing the boy knows for certain, which is that even though she appeared in his yard only this afternoon, and without any tags, they belong to each other. Best friends: that's what they are. He recognized it immediately, as soon as she came trotting over flinging her ears back and forth in the sunlight. Now she sits in the grass cocking her head at him, her pink tongue extending from the slot of her mouth like a Skee-Ball ticket. He runs his hand through her fur. It is white and gray and very soft: feather-duster fur. She has run away from home, he thinks. She has no one to love her but him. His mom and dad are stupid and mean and said, *No. No stray dogs. You can't invite a stray dog into this house,* and he doesn't know if she will be there when he wakes up tomorrow. It hurts, but they both pretend it doesn't. All at once the boy feels the strangest emptiness he has ever felt, as if he hasn't eaten in days and days. It is six o'clock on an orange October night. For a while the insects were clicking and buzzing, and now they are chirping, and the sound is so loud that it's straining the light from the sky. Soon the boy's parents will call him back inside. In his pajamas, while he is supposed to be in bed, he will walk over to the window and watch the dog standing beneath the trees, silently asking for him with the tilt of her brow. After a while she will pad away down the street, her soul newly enclosed in her body, and the boy will go sprinting off into the rest of his childhood, and then his adolescence, and then his life, in search of whoever might give him his own.

EIGHTY-FIVE

A LIFE

There was a skip, like on a record, and she realized she was dead. Her house was still arrayed around her, identical down to the last accoutrement, from the glass jar of seashells in the foyer to the wizened black commas of the candlewicks, but the walls had suddenly become permeable. She found herself seeping through them, flowing silently from room to room. In the kitchen her husband was pouring a midmorning drink for himself, in the bathroom her twelve-year-old was peeing with the door open, and in the stairwell her youngest was playing ricochet with a tennis ball. Oblivious: that's what they were. She filtered back into the master bedroom, where her body lay bunched on the carpet. Forty-three years—my God, so little time! As a girl, convinced she was going to die from whatever cold or fever she had contracted, she used to picture her friends, her parents, her teachers, everyone she knew, rounding their backs in grief over her coffin. For some reason, it was imagining the sobs of her babysitter that always brought her, finally, to tears. To this day she had not lost her sentimental streak. What would they do, her husband and children, she thought. What would they do without her? The impulse must have been all it took, because no sooner had she asked the question than she went welling through the house toward them. Their thoughts, she discovered, were no longer secret to her. She could read them and read them bright. Here was her oldest, flushing the toilet and wincing as he reached for the door: *Sorry. Forgot to close it.* "What's the matter with you? Do you think the whole world wants to watch that?" *Can't even relax in my own house with her around.* And her baby boy, chunking his tennis ball at the wall, then pausing at what sounded like a footstep: *Was that her? Guess not.* "Once and for all, Dustin, will you stop that? How many times do I have to tell you, you're going to leave a mark on the paint." *God. What's the big deal about paint all the time?* And her husband, upending an Irish whiskey to brace himself for the rest of the day: *All right, what? What's wrong now? You know, Lauren, even your smiles look disappointed. Has anyone ever told you that? Okay, wait. Take a deep breath. Be generous. No doubt she tries.* And about that, at least, he was right: she had tried, she really had. But it was too late to say so now. That briary, demanding woman to whom they were all privately speaking—how could that be her? She had always been so confident that she would be missed one day, so certain she was loved. If nothing else, she thought, her life had been a learning experience. But she hadn't wanted a learning experience. She had wanted a life.

EIGHTY-SIX

EXTRAORDINARY GIFTS

That woman in the grocery store who parades down the cereal aisle as if fated to do so, her eyes fixed determinedly forward, is a psychic of extraordinary gifts—not just a mystic performer of the bangles and caftan variety but an authentic spiritual medium. She sees actual ghosts, communes and converses with them. She inherited her abilities from her mother, around whom the ghosts of past generations bobbed as plentifully as cotton in a field. For many years the two of them sat side by side in the candlelit family parlor, conducting mother-daughter séances for gatherings of the bereaved and the curious. When the time came for the mother to die and the daughter to live on, they parted with the confidence of those who know that death is a door that opens both ways. First the psychic was standing over her mother's bed saying, "You look parched, Momma. Let me get you another piece of ice." Then her mother was saying, "I can't see a thing anymore. Oh, honey, this must be it." Then the psychic was whispering, "It's all right. We'll be together again soon." And finally her mother was mustering the strength to nod, giving the barest of yeses before her pillow seemed to swell up around her ears and her soul came rattling out of her body. The psychic had just enough poise to touch her mother's cheek without trembling.

It was a lovely—a perfect—death. Yet at that instant, and ever since, the two of them have faced a predicament, for when the psychic left to call 911 and the coroner, the ghost of her mother, by sheer happenstance, began drifting that way, too. When the psychic went outside to collect the mail, the ghost of her mother, again by sheer happenstance, floated along the paving stones beside her. And later, when the psychic departed for the salon, the ghost of her mother set off along the selfsame path. The situation was decidedly awkward. They had already said their goodbyes, and according to the usual forms of deathbed etiquette, that should have been it. But they could not stop proceeding in matching directions. Every time the psychic tried to peel inconspicuously away, the ghost of her mother had the same idea, slanting off at her side. The longer they failed to acknowledge each other, to wave or salute or say a second bumbling goodbye, the more impossible it seemed to do so.

From that day on, at every turn, the psychic of extraordinary gifts has been chaperoned by the ghost of her mother. She is always on the verge of addressing her, but never so comfortably that she can speak. If, in the grocery store, she pauses stiffly by the energy bars, then swivels around as if she has forgotten something, it is a sign not of grief or eccentricity but of a mind that is elsewhere, anticipating that next and greater death, when she will veer one way and her mother another, at last pursuing their separate courses.

EIGHTY-SEVEN

AN INHERITED DISORDER

From an early age he resolved to be as unlike his father as possible. He was not quite seven when he made up his mind. His father was an alarming giant whose footfalls made the house shake, so he—his son—would be the opposite. At first, his rebellions were fittingly timid. He was quiet where his father was loud, shy where his father was outgoing, sickly where his father was hardy. But slowly, as his father's jurisdiction over him diminished, he grew bolder. Your body, his father liked to say, is God's cathedral, so at eighteen he had God's cathedral pierced, fixing curved silver barbells to his ears, eyebrows, septum, and lower lip. "Live every hour to the fullest" was his father's motto, so he took a job with a consumer research firm, filling out surveys with the inconsequentialia of strangers' buying habits. He married "exactly the kind of fuss-potty boutique shopper" his father despised, raised two children in a way his father found "appallingly laissez-faire," and "foolishly" rented an apartment, rather than "sensibly" investing in a house. Yet these contradistinctions, though genuine, were neither profoundly enough realized, he felt, nor swiftly enough gained. Recently he had noticed the shine of exposed scalp beneath his father's hair: the old man was growing older, and so, for that matter, was he. In this respect, they were just alike.

He decided, therefore, to stop aging. Over the next few years he stayed healthy and young. He was no older a decade later than he had been a decade before. Yet both he and his father, it occurred to him, were still proceeding through time consecutively, tracing the same straight line of minutes and days. Nope. No good. All wrong, he thought. And though it took some doing, after a week or so he began to experience time at a shuffle. One moment he was a twiggy little boy lining his dominoes up on the kitchen floor, the next a surprisingly fit seventy-five-year-old, and the next a high-schooler smoking his very first cigarette. But though his father was experiencing life continuously, and he discontinuously, he was nevertheless, like his father, alive. This wouldn't do at all, he thought, and he relinquished the spark of vitality that imbued him with life. At first all seemed well: he was a ghost, and his father most assuredly was not. Yet it nagged at him, he had to confess, that they both remained singular unified beings—each of them, father and son, himself and himself alone. So rather than being someone in particular, he decided, he would instead be everyone. But as soon as this transition was accomplished— though he was, in fact, everyone (including, he could not deny, his father) and his father was no more than someone—he was disgruntled to realize that both of them still happened or abided, still *eventuated,* squarely within the framework of existence. Whether incarnate or incorporeal, multiple or singular, both he and his father unmistakably *were.* The alternative was obvious. He transformed himself from everyone who was to everything that was not. Finally, he thought, he was as unlike his father as possible, and would remain so until the universe culminated in its own vast nonbeing, into which his father would surely pursue him.

EIGHTY-EIGHT

PRAYER FROM AN AIRPORT TERMINAL

One day a young man of meager religious faith doubted he had the strength to do what was necessary and so decided, against all his instincts, to pray, and to pray as forthrightly as he could: "If there's a God out there who values my well-being, I admit I would be surprised. I can't even say that I actually believe this will work. But I'm praying as sincerely as I know how. I'm speaking, I suppose, not to God, but to anyone who cares enough about me to listen. I'm in trouble. I'm in trouble and I need help. Please help me." As it happened, the ghost of the man's grandfather, like many ghosts, enjoyed eavesdropping now and then on the thoughts of his descendants. Characteristically, he had found, the minds of the living were a confusing ragbag of stray phrases, half-formed wishes, and flickering sense impressions that vibrated with color for barely an instant before they bleached out and disappeared, but every so often one of his children, grandchildren, or great-grandchildren would experience a thought so unmixed that it rose up and penetrated the turmoil. A piece of music could cause it. A strong kiss. A car crash. And that's what the young man's prayer was: a kind of car crash. That the ghost heard it so clearly was a sign of its—the prayer's—desperation. "Help me," the boy kept repeating. "Help me,"

so much fear and pain compressed inside the words that the ghost's sympathy was kindled. Though he was not truly fit to answer prayers—no ghost is—he did what he could, dispatching a warm gust of concentrated emotion into the world: *You'll be all right.* Instantly his grandson felt better. The kindness of his gesture the ghost would never doubt. Its wisdom, though, he soon enough would, for it was upon answering his grandson's prayer that the ghost's difficulties truly began. The problem was that the young man believed he had found God. An unshakable confidence in the power of prayer had been awakened inside him. Two, twelve, fifty times a day, encountering the most mild obstacle or frustration, he would silence all his other thoughts and send out a petition for help, *Dear God this*ing and *Dear God that*ing. "Dear God, please let these trucks get out of the passing lane." "Dear God, please keep the kids from using up the shampoo." Sometimes the ghost was able to soothe his grandson's worries, sometimes not, but whenever his prayers went ignored, the boy became exasperated, mulish, braying more and more loudly for attention. Enough, the ghost thought. Enough of this endless sadness. Enough of this endless pain. Once, instead of transmitting a message of comfort, he tried transmitting a message of aggravation, *Leave me alone,* but this only made matters worse, generating a long procession of neurotic forgive-me prayers. Then and there the ghost realized he was trapped. Imagine it: knowing that for the next fifty or sixty years someone will resort to you and you alone to quench his troubles. He felt the way the junk must feel about the junkie.

EIGHTY-NINE

HATCHING

Not that he truly wished them dead—that wasn't quite it—but more and more often, when the man considered his lifelong friends, his colleagues, even his wife and sons, he felt that their image of him had become so mildewed by habit or complicated by misunderstanding that he took comfort in the idea of their mortality: the thought that soon, very soon, they would die and he would no longer have to be the person they had concluded he was. Instead he himself died—tree branch—which was even better. As a ghost, he was free of all constrictions. If he wanted to bob on the wind like light reflecting from cut glass, he could. If he wanted to trace the path of every capillary on every leaf on every tree in a grove of oaks and birches, he could. Or say he wanted to follow someone and emit a toneless shriek that only he or she could hear, like the squeal of chalk skidmarking across a blackboard—well, he could do that, too. He could be anyone or anything: a statue or a wisp of fog, a sudden slowing of the temperature. And any-*where*, too: on a grassy plain or a busy street corner, a shopping concourse or a Himalayan ridge. He had already been dead some years before he took seriously to haunting people. Often at night, but occasionally in hard daylight, he would arrange himself in the shape he remembered possessing when he was alive, emerging from the air in a ferment of vapors. The families whose homes he visited could never settle among themselves whether he was hostile or benevolent. "All I'm saying is he's never actually *hurt* anybody." "Okay, not yet, but remember when he dashed that mirror to the floor?" "And all those little fires! My God, we're lucky this place hasn't burned to the timbers." "Yes, but who opened the door to let Mr. Whiskers in that night during the snowstorm? *Someone* did, and it wasn't any of you guys." He took pride in the contradictions of his character. They were like the extra limbs he sometimes wore, the additional faces: evidence that he could take whatever form he chose. That was the marrow of it—his contentment, and his malleability, and how the one arose directly from the other. He had finally accepted that this was genuinely his hereafter, and that its pleasures would not simply dissolve away, when, like houseflies laying their eggs, they found him—the ghosts of his friends and family. "That smile of yours," they effused. "And those eyes, so thoughtful and quiet. It's been half a lifetime and look at you: you're exactly the same." They were convinced they had lost him. For decades they had known it as a certainty. But fate had shown them otherwise, and now, they promised, they would never let him out of their sight again. They had missed him, missed him so much, they said. The miracle of it. The blessing.

NINETY

BILATERAL SYMMETRY

By a mishap of circumstance, he died twice in the same instant, his heart seizing just as the alligator snapped its jaws closed around him. Accordingly, his ghost was bisected. On the left side, along with his good ear, was the ghost of the first half of his life. On the right side, along with his tinnitus, was the ghost of the second. He tried for a time to wind himself back together, circumvolving like the stripes of a barber's pole, but eventually he was forced to accept that in this great world of mist and shadows he would never be whole again. His left ghost and his right ghost exchanged their goodbyes, separating to meet their fortunes. Because the first half of his life had been dominated by the many humiliations of love and poverty, his left ghost was restless and unhappy. The best remedy for his dissatisfactions, he soon discovered, was to lose himself in his work. Every ghost who took up haunting had a different specialty. His were the wealthy and the lovestruck: young couples, ideally, luxuriating in an ocean of money and affection. He learned the trick of emerging sideways, slowly, from the giant mirrors in their hotel suites. If he paused just so against his reflection, he could exhibit what looked to careless eyes like the full contours of a human body, half inside the wall and half out. This itself was disturbing enough. But when he broke the symmetry to reveal his spectral cavity—the slick pod of his stomach, the fat maze of his brain—the response he drew from his victims was often profound. The way their screams stair-stepped from fear to genuine horror invigorated him. The second half of the man's life, up until that fateful moment in the Everglades, had been easy, companionable, and secure. As such, his right ghost was remarkably content. He, too, liked to call upon the living, but the hauntings he conducted were recreational rather than professional, a few hours of quiet visitation in the gentle pink of the evening. He became a regular guest at the bed-and-breakfast where he had honeymooned with his second wife. Each afternoon, around the time the insects began to sing, he crossed the mortal border and emerged from behind those damasked walls, relaxing in the scent of potpourri and candles. It wasn't long before his reputation grew wings. Intrepid lovers booked the large southern room on the house's top floor hoping to catch a glimpse of the Welcoming Spirit. They cozied up beneath the covers to wait for sunset, when the space around the sofa would ripple and unfold like the air above a bonfire and an agreeable warmth would rush over the lovers, both erotic and oddly tranquilizing. One night, hunting for someone new to torment, the left ghost happened upon this same bed-and-breakfast. Seeing his other half, he called out in recognition, but in the right ghost's ear there was only the bell of his tinnitus, filling the world with its infinite peal, as strong and as loud as the day he had died.

GHOSTS

✦ AND ✦

WORDS AND NUMBERS

NINETY-ONE

PARAKEETS

Not long ago there lived a man with three pet parakeets: the first appareled in jewel tones of green and yellow, the second with a blue brow that faded into a creamy purple breast, and the third an albino with a beanbag-like belly. Every day from dawn to dusk their chattering permeated the man's sunroom, all blond wood and arched windows. It was the most calming space in the house, his sunroom, but for a single perplexing defect—a frigid patch against the back wall, roughly the size of a water tank. How was it, the man wondered, that even in high summer, at three-thirty in the afternoon, when his shirt was pasted to his back with sweat, he would feel an alarming chill whenever he passed behind the sofa and to the immediate left of the credenza? Sometimes, walking in or out of the room, he would pause before he had emerged from the temperature well just to appreciate the sense of disorientation it caused him: two-thirds of his body warm and comfortable, yet the ice lopping off an arm or a leg, a slice of his foot, the escarpment of his shoulder. One day the man was polishing his hardwoods when, to access a section of the floor, he moved the birdcage into the cold patch. A silence enshrouded the birds. Their feathers flattened. Whether through tiredness or simple absentmindedness, the man neglected to restore the cage to its spot in the corner, and by the next morning, when he returned, the perches and wires were covered in a verdigris of frost. As he approached, the parakeets stood at attention. Try as he might, he had never been able to extend their vocabulary beyond a few basic words: *birdseed, not-now, pretty-bird, night-night*. Yet now, so quietly he would not have heard them if the air conditioner had not clicked off, the first bird said, "I do not know where I am." And the second bird said, "I deserve another chance." And "The wind here is so bitter and it never stops," said the albino. The man felt as if someone had emptied a breath onto the nape of his neck. A marshy smell rose from his armpits. He had always enjoyed riddles, even insoluble ones, but there were riddles and then there were riddles. He instructed himself to move the cage back to the corner. *Do it. Do it.* But the cold of the copper bit his fingers to the skeleton. He flinched. He backed away. Without thinking, because he had said it so many times before, he asked, "Who's a pretty bird?" The parakeets eyed him with a daunting directness. "Is someone there? Will you speak up? Let us out. Come closer. I can almost hear you. Come closer. Come closer. Let us out." Between the bars of the cage everything was green and yellow like the grass at daybreak, or blue and violet like the last brush of the evening, or fat and white like the sun pinned in the sky, until he reached for the latch and the darkness rushed in.

NINETY-TWO

EUPHEMISMS

In the village of which we speak, bordered by mountain folds forested with vine-draped trees, everything was a euphemism for something else. The villagers laughed and cried, but it was not what they meant. They fell in love and out again, but it was not what they meant. They told jokes, and visited the doctor, and celebrated birthdays, and attended weddings and baby showers, and they woke with hangovers, and they gossiped with their neighbors, and they watched the rain douse their window screens and the sun play keno with the mesh squares afterward, but none of it was what they really meant. One might think that in such a place, so ruled by circumlocutions and genteelisms, life would be impossible, an impenetrable tangle of codes and mysteries, but in fact the villagers understood each other perfectly well, for it was not a million different somethings they could not bring themselves to acknowledge but a single, conflagrating something, unified and elemental, which cast its light over them like the midday sun. They behaved as though a peck on the cheek meant a peck on the cheek, a physics lecture meant a physics lecture, a gardener plucking weeds from his vegetables meant a gardener plucking weeds from his vegetables, but in reality they knew better, since the peck, the lecture, and the gardening all concealed the same harsh truth, which, though widely understood, indeed swaying on the tip of every tongue, remained not only unexpressed but inexpressible. On those rare occasions when one of them tried to speak of it directly, the response was immediate. The others would meet him with a tucked-away look of nervous disgust, the muscles working around their eyes, but barely, in twitches, as if they were trying to remain dignified in spite of some great pain. They need not have worried. A protective internal mechanism always swung into place to guide such blunderers into the usual benign substitutions, into speaking as if every word possessed one meaning and one alone, which was too obvious to be questioned. Only the most careful examination revealed the tension behind their exchanges. Occasionally, when the villagers asked "How's life been treating you?" or "Work going well?" they did so with a brief delay. Sometimes their smiles looked as if they had been tugged into place by an invisible stitch. At moments it seemed for all the world as if they were gazing back, regretfully, on a life that had already passed. There are two kinds of being. This was the other one.

NINETY-THREE

ROUGHLY EIGHTY GRAMS

In a once fashionable but now neglected area of the city stood a Chinese restaurant known for the ghost who haunted it. Like many ghosts she was a creature of wild mood swings, all bitter inwardness and tortured amours. The daughter of the restaurant's hostess and its chef, she had spent a short, jilted life crying in the upstairs apartment, making sad small-animal sounds that filtered down onto the tables and bamboo partitions, audible even over the burble of the aquarium. Her agonies, her histrionics—to her mother and father they were embarrassing. So disobedient. So American. And now, to their equal embarrassment, she was spending her afterlife inside the restaurant itself, romancing every handsome male diner between the ages of fifteen and forty. As an inducement she liked to replace the fortunes in their cookies with declarations of love. The men cracked the cookies open expecting, say, "A chance meeting opens new doors to success," and instead, in blue type on white paper, got, "Your laugh makes me feel like the grass must feel when the wind blows through it," or "You may think it's been extinguished, but I can see the fire in your eyes," or "When will you hold me in your strong, sunburned arms?" Worse, her parents thought, she was becoming less affectionate over time, less lyrical; more acrid, impatient, wounded, angry, envious.

"If you don't love me, why pretend?" she wrote, or "That girl of yours—her eye wanders," or "Make up your mind, because I will not wait forever."

When she began terrorizing the restaurant, and not just haunting it, was a matter of some debate among the customers. Everyone agreed, though, that after she fell in love with the man who coached peewee soccer in the weedy field behind the storage center, there was no turning back. Twice a week following practice, sometime around six o'clock, the man would come into the restaurant with his girlfriend and order the Crispy Fried Tofu with Spicy Pepper Salt. "I want to crawl inside your clothing with you," his fortunes always said, or "I want to taste the ginger of your sweat on my tongue." He found the blunt seductiveness of these messages amusing, even a little thrilling, and so, when it came to it, did his girlfriend. "Daffy" was the word she used. But for her, each meal in the restaurant swiftly degenerated into a series of lesser mishaps. The rooster sauce would not leave the bottle for her, and then left it all at once. Water glasses toppled and spilled onto her blouse. Her food reached the table sputtering with heat, except for the soups, which were cold as slush. And slowly the fortunes in the man's cookies became more insulting. "She is not perfect, she only looks perfect." "She is not good enough for you." "You would not love her if her flesh were as ruined as her heart." "Here. Watch. I will show you." It was the night of their last meal in the restaurant, just after the check arrived, that the man's girlfriend excused herself to use the restroom. Not a minute later her scream came. At first the man mistook it for a train braking, so shrill was the sound, and so ragged. He had already taken his cookie from the wrapper, but was reluctant to break it open. It weighed too much.

NINETY-FOUR

THE GHOST LETTER

$k\}l$

In April, the U.S. secretary of philology held a press confer-
ence to announce the discovery of a twenty-seventh letter,
dead for some centuries, that had been haunting the alphabet
at least since the time of Cervantes. Formerly, the secretary
said, the letter was located between *k* and *l*. While its shape
and sound were lost to history, it was believed to have been a
consonant rather than a vowel. There was no evidence that its
current aims, unascertained though they may be, were perni-
cious or occult. One of the journalists present called it "the
ghost letter," as in "What does the president have to say about
this ghost letter?" and the name quickly seized the public's
imagination. Within days, an effort began to determine which
words housed the ghost letter and which did not, and whether,
contrary to the official posture, those that did gave off an aura
of ill will. The results were inconclusive. Fewer words contained the letter than didn't—far fewer—but the same could
be said of every letter, *a* and *e* included. Among the words that
possessed it, in one hidden berth or another, were *waistband,
learning, potato, glandular, ask, inadvertent,* and *noggin.* Maybe
there was a common variable in this catalogue, but if so, it
was elusive. And what of such similar words as *ruddy,* which
sheltered the letter, and *reddish,* which did not; *stripe,* which

did, and *striping,* which did not; even *record* (a list), which did, and *record* (to write down), which did not? An analysis of the most exalted authors of the last hundred years showed that a surprising number of them had inclined toward the ghostly, making of their books, as if by intuition, a veritable golgotha of haunted words, but it was hard to tell if the otherworldly quality people now attributed to their writing was genuine or an illusion. By what force did their work take its turn toward the uncanny? That was the question. Student novelists began seeding their manuscripts with the same phantom words the masters had used, believing that the right tumble of syllables might lend their prose a luster of greatness, while evangelists and conservative politicians scrubbed the same identical checklist of words from their sermons and speeches. To some the twenty-seventh letter whispered of the wondrous, to others of the monstrous. The great shared regret was that no one knew how it had died: violently or peacefully. Clearly what was needed—and absent a body could never be achieved—was a postmortem, one that might determine whether the letter had succumbed to old age or been murdered. And if it had been murdered, by whom? And which letter might be next?

NINETY-FIVE

A MATTER OF LINGUISTICS

A feeling of déjà vu has been gaining on him all morning, but only now, waiting in the hotel's lobby for the thunderstorm to pass, does he succumb to it. The couch on which he is sitting—he is certain he has sat there before. The upholstery button beneath his trousers, hard and bulbous like a walnut shell—the word, he believes, is "goosed." It has goosed him before. Each fat raindrop that strikes the skylight makes an amoeba-like shadow on the floor, trembling little off-round ghosts that come and go in spatters. He imagines the shadows are pinned beneath the slide of a microscope, and he along with them, flat. He has heard these raindrops before. He has imagined himself beneath that microscope. Along with his déjà vu comes a curious tightening sensation, like a charley horse, except intellectual rather than physical. A charley horse of the brain. He is disappointed in something, and that something, he realizes, is language. The man in the hotel's lobby is, as it happens, a linguist of some accomplishment, on the board of *Semios* and *Metalinguistics* and the founding editor of *Verb Studies*. He has devoted his career to words, to their codes and systems. Yet he is—he ceaselessly at this moment has been—disillusioned with language. Yes, yes, it is a dazzling spectacle, he can't disagree, he has said it many times himself. But it lacks the malleability of real experience. The most ordinary prose might be a great sequence of parse trees combusting from brochures and assembly instructions, shopping circulars and term papers, like a display of fireworks—but so what? Where, he thinks, is the verb tense that could convey his feeling of déjà vu, the conviction that everything that is happening to him has happened before, and happened to its completion? Call it the present super-perfect. He decides here and now, never before but not for the first time, that he will concoct such a tense. He will start with the present singular, sand the difficulties away, then move on to the plural, the past, and the future. He will make it his professional mission to introduce the tense into the vernacular. Despite his institutional prominence, his frequent public radio appearances, his lengthy CV of grants and residencies, what he longs for most of all is to make a true creative contribution to his field. He wants to change the language, to improve it. Not analysis, not heraldry. Invention. Someday, he thinks, everyone will be capable of speaking in the most casual way of living their life as though they are remembering it, and philologists the world over will celebrate the moment when the linguist sat listening to the rain detonate against the asphalt and began to understand what he has just now come always to have suspected.

NINETY-SIX

DUSK AND OTHER STORIES

When the poltergeist realized he could communicate only through telekinesis, he succumbed to a period of humiliation. He, a man of eloquence and culture, whose first pleasure had always been good conversation, and now look at him, dickering with the lights and the faucets. It was degrading! For several decades he lay as quiet as paint inside the house. Once or twice a year he would flow through the carpet to feel its fibers dance and reassure himself that he still existed, but otherwise he held his peace. Better to remain silent, he judged, than resort to hiding keys, flinging crockery, and all that nonsense. Then, however, the house was sold to a widower, recently retired from publishing, who bricked its walls over with his ten thousand books, and the poltergeist perceived an opportunity. One afternoon, while the widower was sitting in his armchair, the poltergeist withdrew a book partway from the nearest case. *Listen to Me* was the title. The widower shifted slightly inside his posture, then got up and squared the book away, carefully neatening it with both his thumbs. Again the poltergeist gave it a tug: *Listen to Me.* From two shelves down he chose a second book: *Look at Me.* Next to it was a novel called *The Household Spirit,* and for good measure the poltergeist loosened that one too. This was how their dialogue began, and the medium through which it developed. Gradually the edges of certain books became soft from use. The poltergeist had studied the widower's library, memorizing every title until their positions shone like stars on a star chart. It was easy for him to say good night to the widower with *After Dark,* good morning with *Greetings from Earth.* But he was also adept at combining titles when he wanted to speak more complexly, or more elliptically. The widower noticed that the philodendron near his science fiction collection was browning, and *The Dazzle of Day,* the poltergeist suggested. *Summerlong. Dying Inside.* Patting his hair into place, the widower complained about his bald spot. The poltergeist answered, *Boy Erased,* then slid another title teasingly out of plumb: *Calamities.* "I wish I had someone who would outlast me," the widower said. "Other than you, I mean. No offense." *The Beautiful Indifference.* "A daughter, a son. Even a pet." *Beasts and Children.* "But as usual I'm all wrapped up in my own problems. What about you? How are you doing this morning?" *All the Days and Nights. Everything We Miss.* "Is that so?" the widower said. "Well, I'm sorry to hear it." One summer, some five years into their friendship, the widower began to feel firm in places where he had always been soft. When eventually the diagnosis came, he confessed that he was afraid. The poltergeist followed him as he perambulated through the house. No one who is dying ever really asks for the consolations of the spirit, but as the widower paused for breath in his study the poltergeist told him *The Sweet Hereafter* and *A Reunion of Ghosts.* By the front door he continued *What the Living Do, The Other Side of the Mountain,* and *Death as a Side Effect.* In the nook beside the kitchen he reassured him *I Will Not Leave You Comfortless.* And in the guest room, with the firmest of tugs, he said *Drag the Darkness Down.*

NINETY-SEVEN

TELEPHONE

They were friends by proximity rather than choice: she almost nine, a self-proclaimed tomboy and motormouth, he ten and a half, soft-spoken and bookish, with the dawdliness of a born daydreamer. Their bedroom windows faced each other over a chain-link fence and an old steel air conditioner so that at night, or on certain rainy days, their lives were spent side by side at a distance of approximately eight feet. This alone was enough to make them friends. Add to that the scarcity of other children on the block—aside from the two of them there was only one sausage-like baby in the duplex across the street—and they became almost inseparable. The two of them fashioned a telephone out of yogurt cups and kite string, a makeshift apparatus that worked surprisingly well. Often, at bedtime, in the twenty minutes or so before they dozed off, they would chat idly along the line—or rather she would chat and he would throw in an occasional *mm-hm* or *uh-huh* to keep her going. Eventually one of two things would always happen: either he would fall asleep and she would keep talking for a while, her speech culminating in a few hellos? and a prodigious yawn; or *she* would fall asleep and he would freeze suddenly beneath his covers, becoming so still, so quiet, that his body prickled with quills of nervous concentration, and lying there in the darkness, caught in the net of his muscles, he would listen for the voice of the ghost. It was languorous and heavy, that voice, almost expressionless, and unlike the girl's in every way. That it was a ghost's was merely his guess, since it never replied when he asked it a question, only shrank into silence, emerging hesitantly, in flickers, after many minutes if at all. He could feel its syllables landing one by one against the wall of his skull. They were like ocean waves from some planet where the water was as thick as syrup. *Where–is–the–noise–of–you–coming–from? The–air–is–like–salt–in–side–me.* One night, frightened but worried, the boy summoned up enough courage to approach his window and peer across the gap. The girl had not drawn her curtains. He saw her sleeping beneath her favorite puppy sheets, nuzzling a strand of brown hair in her lips, safe in her ordinary room, with its ordinary toybox, its ordinary bookcase, its ordinary dresser. Her end of the telephone lay in a little dell between her pillow and her shoulder. Plain sight told him that no one was using it. Yet still the ghost murmured in his ear, *Are–you–out–there? There–are–bells–in–the–ice. They–ring–so–loud–and–you–are–pain–full–y–qui–et.* Years later, grown up, the boy would come to believe that in a fever of boredom or abnormality he had simply dreamed the voice into being, but standing there at the window he had no doubt that it was real. The ghost was his friend, too, he supposed, not by proximity but by the vicissitudes of death, connected to him by some infinitely long kite string, some preternatural yogurt cup.

NINETY-EIGHT

NUMBERS

╫╫
|||

Six billion four thousand and forty-one. Six billion four thousand and forty-two. Six billion four thousand and forty-three. The boy was still in the cradle when he began hearing the numbers, far too young to recognize them for what they were. To his ears they were just one of the many sounds the world produced, an almost subaudible buzz of enumeration that came and went with the hours, like the hello-calls of the birds and the insects, or the bending noises the trees made in the wind. Nature creaked, nature rustled, nature chirped, and nature counted. It was a fact, as ordinary as any other. He was halfway through elementary school before it occurred to him that the numbers he was multiplying and dividing in his workbook were like the numbers that helped him fall asleep at night. He was not stupid, or at least he did not think he was, but until then the similarity had never crossed his mind. The original numbers—the world's numbers, as he thought of them—were simply too familiar. All his life he had been conscious of their background presence, their whisperiness, the way they stopped and started and stopped again. For a while they would proceed sequentially. Then softly, unassumingly, they would break off. After a while they would recommence, but always at a different point in the series, either much later or much earlier, swooping from the high billions to the low thousands and back again. Not until college did the boy realize that not everyone could hear them. One day, in the dorm's cafeteria, he noticed that the digits were swiftly approaching a million. Nine hundred ninety-nine thousand nine hundred and ninety-four. Nine hundred ninety-nine thousand nine hundred and ninety-five. He hushed his friends, said, "Hold on, are you ready?" and then, after a few seconds, made a presto motion with his finger. From their expressions, as flat as doors, he understood that they were deaf to the recitation. It was like discovering that he and he alone was aware of the seasons. A million and six. A million and seven. A million and eight. As the boy grew older, he began to sense that each act of counting belonged to a different voice—that he was listening to many distinct and ongoing monologues rather than a single sporadic one. Each voice had its own personality, each personality its own numbers. Maybe he was overhearing the lifetime tally of people's footsteps. Maybe some strange cellular background calculation. There were so many possibilities. He always believed he would solve the puzzle before he died. Then he did die, and at first he was none the wiser. He found himself standing in a great landscape of ghosts, epochs and epochs of them, stretching in all directions. They were locked like pillars into their stances, the ghosts, frozen exactly where they had expired. Between their teeth they were mumbling something. What was he supposed to do? he wondered. What did it mean? He was preparing to ask the question when his lips began moving, and quietly, fixed in his eternal place, he heard himself take up his obligation. One. Two. Three. Four.

NINETY-NINE

THE CENSUS

On the day of the Divine Census, when, as was His custom, God brought the world to a halt to conduct a head count, He discovered to His alarm that the imaginary beings outnumbered the real ones. Always before their sums had been exactly the same, soul for soul and integer for integer. For every elf, ghost, yeti, doppelgänger, mermaid, fairy, or elemental, there was a person of flesh and blood, and for every person of flesh and blood, there was an elf, ghost, yeti, etc. This was the hidden equation that held the world together, dating back to the days of Adam (real), Eve (real), Satan (imaginary), and Lilith (who for just that reason had been obliged to become a demon, and thus imaginary). Alter the balance in either direction, God knew, and Creation would spill out of itself like a raindrop; He was surprised, frankly, that it hadn't already. Acting from the most abundant caution, He took a second tally. The discrepancy was still apparent. There was no such thing as a trivial incongruity when it came to the Census—one was equal to one, always and absolutely. Still, a half-dozen dryads and a gremlin or two He might have understood. In this case, though, the numbers were completely out of whack, differing not just by the hundreds but by the hundreds of thousands. Clearly, He had some work to do. And so, like the watchmaker people so frequently supposed Him to be, He began making minute adjustments to the machinery of reality, twisting various pieces to render actual beings fictitious and fictitious beings actual. He started by restoring the ghosts to life, but this tipped the scales of existence too far toward the material. So He transformed a few of the living back into ghosts—first the Omars and then, when the totals still were not even, the Sallys. After each new tweak He performed another calculation, watching from above as people retrieved and lost their human lines. All this ghostliness, He determined, was getting Him nowhere. So He turned His hand to the angels and the giants, the trolls and archbishops, to child stars, forest gnomes, commodities traders between the ages of thirty-six and thirty-seven. Figures both plain and fantastic either waned out of existence or budded into it. Finally their numbers were nearly identical, with only a two-being difference in favor of the real. The solution was obvious. With a gentle flourish of His will, God rearranged Himself from a genuine figure into an imaginary one. At once, and thenceforward, the world pursued its course unwittingly, intrinsically, and independently—without, that is to say, Him. The majority of theologians regard this as His most impressive feat to date.

THE MOST TERRIFYING
GHOST STORY EVER WRITTEN

The most terrifying ghost story ever written originated in an obscure pocket dialect of the Himalayas in the middle years of the nineteenth century. It entered the English-speaking world in 1898, when the Canadian missionary to whom it had been entrusted some twenty years earlier published a translation with L. C. Page & Company under the title "The Devouring Mask of Nanqi Zhang." In an afterword, the missionary noted that the stone and cedar village that had birthed the manuscript once harbored roughly three hundred inhabitants, a spare dozen of whom were lettered enough to write, though by 1895, he said, when he attempted a second visit, it had been abandoned altogether, the houses engulfed by the scree and the dirt. At first the volume sold modestly. A 1937 screen adaptation, however, starring Luise Rainer and Fredric March, and released as "A Ghost in the Hills," brought an enduring cult celebrity to the tale. It has remained in print ever since, issued by a half-dozen distinct presses, under a half-dozen disparate titles, and in a half-dozen independent yet bizarrely matching translations. By 1960, when the book's copyright lapsed, the eldritch dramatics of its style were considered quaint if not downright fusty, so an editor at Farrar, Straus & Cudahy commissioned a new translation. The professor who undertook the project declined to consult the missionary's edition, working instead from a photostat of the original manuscript. No one, he claimed, was more surprised by the result than he. Every sentence, every paragraph, had come out exactly the same. It seemed impossible, yet the new edition, released to much fanfare, was interchangeable with the first. Only the title differentiated it: what had been "The Devouring Mask of Nanqi Zhang" was now, by editorial fiat, "Widowman Chu and the Whisper in the Night." Since then, five more translations have followed, each produced without recourse to any of the earlier efforts but identical down to the last comma, the last subordinate clause, except for the titles: *The Woodcutter and the Snow Woman, The Dark Maw of the Forest, Into My Arms, Into My Teeth, For I Will Drink Your Blood Like Water,* and, most recently, *Why, Darling, Why.* Though the translators have adopted a variety of working practices, ranging from the metaphrastic to the idiomatic, each of them has reported feeling, upon turning their pen to the material, as if their intentions had been swallowed by some greater force. There may be some truth to this assertion. For the fact is that despite the book's grizzled plot and the weaknesses of its prose, it has garnered more acclaim with each new publication. Scholars have suggested that it may be the first text in history impervious not to translation but to change.

A Partial Concordance of Themes

GHOSTS AND ANIMALS Fourteen. Elephants, Fifteen. The White Mare, Sixteen. Many Additional Animals, Seventeen. Bees, Twenty-nine. Minnows, Thirty. A Story Swaying Back and Forth, Thirty-nine. There Are People, They Had Lives, Forty-six. Playtime, Eighty-four. A Second True Story, Ninety-one. Parakeets

GHOSTS AND PLANTS Eighteen. A Blight on the Landscape, Nineteen. An Ossuary of Trees, Twenty. Things That Fall from the Sky, Twenty-one. A Story with a Drum Beating Inside It, Twenty-three. Renewable Resources, Thirty. A Story Swaying Back and Forth, Forty-six. Playtime

GHOSTS AND SOLITUDE Two. The Guidance Counselor, Twelve. A Gathering, Twenty-nine. Minnows, Thirty-six. A Blackness Went Fluttering By, Forty-five. The Walls, Forty-nine. A Story Seen in Glimpses Through the Mist, Fifty-four. Bouquet, Fifty-five. The Mud Odor of the Snow Melting in the Fields, Sixty-three. Which Are the Crystals, Which the Solution, Sixty-nine. The Apostrophes, Seventy. A Man in a Mirror, Ninety-three. Roughly Eighty Grams

GHOSTS AND COMPANIONSHIP Five. Amnesia, Twelve. A Gathering, Thirty-one. A Time-Travel Story with a Little Romance and a Happy Ending, Thirty-eight. His Womanhood, Forty-three. Spectrum, Forty-four. Every House Key, Every Fire Hydrant, Every Electrical Outlet, Fifty-two. So Many Songs, Fifty-four. Bouquet, Fifty-six. Instrumentology, Fifty-seven. When the Room Is Quiet, the Daylight Almost Gone, Sixty-seven. Lost and Found, Sixty-nine. The Apostrophes,

Seventy-one. Turnstiles, Seventy-two. A True Story, Seventy-four. Knees, Seventy-seven. Too Late, Seventy-eight. Detention, Seventy-nine. I Like Your Shoes, Eighty-three. Ghost Brothers, Eighty-four. A Second True Story, Eighty-six. Extraordinary Gifts, Eighty-nine. Hatching, Ninety-three. Roughly Eighty Grams, Ninety-six. Dusk and Other Stories

GHOSTS AND HEARTBREAK One. A Notable Social Event, Sixty-three. Which Are the Crystals, Which the Solution, Sixty-eight. Another Man in a Mirror, Seventy. A Man in a Mirror, Seventy-two. A True Story, Seventy-three. Bullets and What It Takes to Dodge Them, Seventy-five. The Man She Is Trying to Forget, Seventy-six. The Eternities, Seventy-seven. Too Late, Eighty-five. A Life, Ninety-three. Roughly Eighty Grams

GHOSTS AND CHILDHOOD Twenty-seven. The Midpoint, Thirty-one. A Time-Travel Story with a Little Romance and a Happy Ending, Forty-four. Every House Key, Every Fire Hydrant, Every Electrical Outlet, Forty-six. Playtime, Forty-seven. All His Life, Fifty-seven. When the Room Is Quiet, the Daylight Almost Gone, Sixty-seven. Lost and Found, Seventy-eight. Detention, Eighty-one. A Source of Confusion, Eighty-two. Unseeable, Untouchable, Eighty-three. Ghost Brothers, Eighty-four. A Second True Story, Ninety-seven. Telephone

GHOSTS AND OLD AGE Twenty-seven. The Midpoint, Forty-five. The Walls, Fifty. A Lifetime of Touch, Fifty-two. So Many Songs, Fifty-four. Bouquet, Seventy-three. Bullets and What It Takes to Dodge Them, Eighty. The Ghost's Disguise, Ninety-six. Dusk and Other Stories

GHOSTS AND FAMILY Eighty. The Ghost's Disguise, Eighty-one. A Source of Confusion, Eighty-five. A Life, Eighty-six. Extraordinary

GHOSTS AND ART Forty-three. Spectrum, Fifty. A Lifetime of Touch, Sixty-two. Real Estate

GHOSTS AND MUSIC Twenty-one. A Story with a Drum Beating Inside It, Fifty-one. The Runner-Up, Fifty-two. So Many Songs, Fifty-six. Instrumentology

GHOSTS AND LITERATURE Thirty-one. A Time-Travel Story with a Little Romance and a Happy Ending, Ninety-four. The Ghost Letter, Ninety-six. Dusk and Other Stories, One Hundred. The Most Terrifying Ghost Story Ever Written

GHOSTS AND FILM Thirteen. Mira Amsler, Forty-one. Action!, Eighty-two. Unseeable, Untouchable

GHOSTS AND ECOLOGY Twelve. A Gathering, Eighteen. A Blight on the Landscape, Nineteen. An Ossuary of Trees, Twenty-two. The Sandbox Initiative, Twenty-three. Renewable Resources, Thirty-four. Passengers

GHOSTS AND LANGUAGE Four. Milo Krain, Eight. Wishes, Ninety-one. Parakeets, Ninety-two. Euphemisms, Ninety-three. Roughly Eighty Grams, Ninety-four. The Ghost Letter, Ninety-five. A Matter of Linguistics, Ninety-seven. Telephone, One Hundred. The Most Terrifying Ghost Story Ever Written

GHOSTS AND THE SENSES Fourteen. Elephants, Nineteen. An Ossuary of Trees, Twenty. Things That Fall from the Sky, Thirty-seven. The Prism, Forty. The Soldiers of the 115th Regiment, Forty-two. The Way the Ring of a Moat Becomes Comforting to a Fish, Forty-three. Spectrum, Forty-four. Every House Key, Every Fire Hydrant, Every Electrical Outlet, Forty-eight. Take It with Me, Forty-nine. A Story

The Office of Hereafters and Dissolutions, Thirty-three. Footprints, Thirty-four. Passengers, Thirty-seven. The Prism, Forty. The Soldiers of the 115th Regiment, Forty-six. Playtime, Fifty-one. The Runner-Up, Fifty-seven. When the Room Is Quiet, the Daylight Almost Gone, Fifty-nine. A Lesser Feeling, Sixty-two. Real Estate, Sixty-three. Which Are the Crystals, Which the Solution, Sixty-four. Countless Strange Couplings and Separations, Sixty-five. Rapture, Sixty-six. 666, Sixty-eight. Another Man in a Mirror, Sixty-nine. The Apostrophes, Seventy. A Man in a Mirror, Seventy-seven. Too Late, Eighty-five. A Life, Eighty-six. Extraordinary Gifts, Eighty-eight. Prayer from an Airport Terminal, Eighty-nine. Hatching, Ninety-one. Parakeets, Ninety-three. Roughly Eighty Grams, Ninety-eight. Numbers

GHOSTS AND THE FEELING THAT ONE MIGHT JUST AS WELL LIE DOWN AND NEVER GET UP AGAIN One. A Notable Social Event, Twenty-eight. The Whirl of Time, Forty-one. Action!, Fifty-five. The Mud Odor of the Snow Melting in the Fields, Fifty-seven. When the Room Is Quiet, the Daylight Almost Gone, Sixty-four. Countless Strange Couplings and Separations, Seventy-two. A True Story

GHOSTS AND THAT FEELING YOU GET IN YOUR THIRTIES AND FORTIES, AND OCCASIONALLY EVEN INTO YOUR FIFTIES, THAT YOU ARE LOST IN A BOAT AT SEA, AND THE STORM IS MAKING WAVES AS TALL AS HOUSES, AND YOU ARE JUST WAITING FOR THE BOARDS TO COME APART, AND THOUGH SOMETIMES THE STORM MIGHT SUBSIDE AND THE WATER SUDDENLY SEEM LIKE GLASS TO YOU—AND MAYBE THAT IS A LITTLE BETTER—YOU ARE STILL IN THE MIDDLE OF THE OCEAN AFTER ALL, AND YOU DON'T SEEM TO BE GOING ANYWHERE, AND THE ONLY SOLUTION THAT ACTUALLY OCCURS TO YOU IS TO TAKE OUT A GUN AND BLOW A HOLE IN THE BOTTOM OF THE BOAT Two. The Guidance Counselor, Sixty-three. Which Are the

Lives, Forty-two. The Way the Ring of a Moat Becomes Comforting to a Fish, Fifty-six. Instrumentology, Eighty-two. Unseeable, Untouchable, Eighty-seven. An Inherited Disorder, One Hundred. The Most Terrifying Ghost Story Ever Written

GHOSTS AND ACCELERATION Twenty-four. Thirteen Visitations, Twenty-seven. The Midpoint, Twenty-eight. The Whirl of Time, Thirty-two. The Phantasm vs. the Statue, Forty-seven. All His Life, Seventy-three. Bullets and What It Takes to Dodge Them

GHOSTS AND STASIS One. A Notable Social Event, Six. A Long Chain of Yesterdays, Twenty-eight. The Whirl of Time, Thirty. A Story Swaying Back and Forth, Thirty-two. The Phantasm vs. the Statue, Thirty-six. A Blackness Went Fluttering By, Forty-nine. A Story Seen in Glimpses Through the Mist, Sixty-three. Which Are the Crystals, Which the Solution, Sixty-eight. Another Man in a Mirror, Seventy-six. The Eternities, Ninety-eight. Numbers

GHOSTS AND PSYCHIC PHENOMENA Fifteen. The White Mare, Forty-three. Spectrum, Forty-four. Every House Key, Every Fire Hydrant, Every Electrical Outlet, Fifty-three. A Matter of Acoustics, Fifty-four. Bouquet, Sixty-two. Real Estate, Eighty-six. Extraordinary Gifts, Ninety-seven. Telephone, Ninety-eight. Numbers

GHOSTS AND SOCIAL AWKWARDNESS One. A Notable Social Event, Nine. How to Play, Fifty-six. Instrumentology, Sixty-three. Which Are the Crystals, Which the Solution, Sixty-nine. The Apostrophes, Seventy-five. The Man She Is Trying to Forget, Seventy-nine. I Like Your Shoes, Eighty-one. A Source of Confusion, Eighty-five. A Life, Eighty-six. Extraordinary Gifts, Eighty-seven. An Inherited Disorder, Eighty-eight. Prayer from an Airport Terminal, Eighty-nine. Hatching, Ninety-two. Euphemisms

Passengers, Thirty-six. A Blackness Went Fluttering By, Forty-one. Action!, Sixty-five. Rapture, Eighty-one. A Source of Confusion

GHOSTS AND THE POSSIBLE Nineteen. An Ossuary of Trees, Thirty-one. A Time-Travel Story with a Little Romance and a Happy Ending, Forty-five. The Walls, Fifty-one. The Runner-Up, Sixty-one. The Abnormalist and the Usualist, Sixty-eight. Another Man in a Mirror, Seventy-two. A True Story, Seventy-five. The Man She Is Trying to Forget, Eighty-two. Unseeable, Untouchable, Ninety-five. A Matter of Linguistics

GHOSTS AND THE DIMLY POSSIBLE BUT HIGHLY UNLIKELY Fourteen. Elephants, Thirty-eight. His Womanhood, Forty-one. Action!, Fifty-two. So Many Songs, One Hundred. The Most Terrifying Ghost Story Ever Written

✦

One A Notable Social Event → Heartbreak, the Past, the Unlucky, Never Getting Up Again, Memory, Repetitions, Stasis, Social Awkwardness

Two The Guidance Counselor → Solitude, Blowing a Hole in the Bottom of the Boat, Memory, School Life

Three A Hatchet, Several Candlesticks, a Pincushion, and a Top Hat → Storytelling, Houses, Memory, Duplications, Multiplicity

Four Milo Krain → Language, the Unlucky, Forgetfulness

Five Amnesia → Companionship, the Past, Forgetfulness

Seventeen Bees → Animals, Balance

Eighteen A Blight on the Landscape → Plants, Balance, Ecology, the Unlucky, Repetitions, Multiplicity

Nineteen An Ossuary of Trees → Plants, Storytelling, Houses, Ecology, the Senses, the Possible

Twenty Things That Fall from the Sky → Plants, the Senses, the Lucky, Multiplicity

Twenty-one A Story with a Drum Beating Inside It → Plants, Balance, Music, the Lucky

Twenty-two The Sandbox Initiative → Technology, Ecology, Memory

Twenty-three Renewable Resources → Plants, Time, Technology, Ecology, the Future, the Unlucky

Twenty-four Thirteen Visitations → Time, Houses, Forgetfulness, Acceleration

Twenty-five The Office of Hereafters and Dissolutions → Time, Imbalance, Numbers, Borrowed Stories, the Unlucky

Twenty-six An Obituary → Time, Imbalance, the Past

Twenty-seven The Midpoint → Childhood, Old Age, Time, Balance, the Past, the Future, Duplications, Acceleration

Twenty-eight The Whirl of Time → Time, the Future, Never Getting Up Again, Acceleration, Stasis

Thirty-nine There Are People, They Had Lives → Animals, Space, Imbalance, Duplications, Multiplicity

Forty The Soldiers of the 115th Regiment → Time, the Senses, the Unlucky, Memory

Forty-one Action! → Film, Never Getting Up Again, the Apocalypse, the Dimly Possible but Highly Unlikely

Forty-two The Way the Ring of a Moat Becomes Comforting to a Fish → Balance, the Senses, Duplications, Singularity

Forty-three Spectrum → Companionship, Color, Art, the Senses, Psychic Phenomena, School Life, Multiplicity

Forty-four Every House Key, Every Fire Hydrant, Every Electrical Outlet → Companionship, Childhood, Houses, the Senses, Psychic Phenomena, Multiplicity

Forty-five The Walls → Solitude, Old Age, Numbers, Houses, the Past, Multiplicity, the Possible

Forty-six Playtime → Animals, Plants, Childhood, the Unlucky, Forgetfulness, Multiplicity

Forty-seven All His Life → Childhood, the Lucky, Acceleration, School Life

Forty-eight Take It with Me → Balance, Color, the Senses

Forty-nine A Story Seen in Glimpses Through the Mist → Solitude, Space, the Senses, Stasis

A PARTIAL CONCORDANCE OF THEMES

Sixty-two Real Estate → Space, the Bible, Houses, Art, the Unlucky, Psychic Phenomena

Sixty-three Which Are the Crystals, Which the Solution → Solitude, Heartbreak, Imbalance, the Unlucky, Blowing a Hole in the Bottom of the Boat, Stasis, Social Awkwardness

Sixty-four Countless Strange Couplings and Separations → Space, the Senses, the Unlucky, Never Getting Up Again, Multiplicity

Sixty-five Rapture → The Bible, the Unlucky, the Apocalypse

Sixty-six 666 → Space, Numbers, the Bible, Houses, the Unlucky, Multiplicity

Sixty-seven Lost and Found → Companionship, Childhood, Imbalance

Sixty-eight Another Man in a Mirror → Heartbreak, the Unlucky, Blowing a Hole in the Bottom of the Boat, Reflections, Stasis, the Possible

Sixty-nine The Apostrophes → Solitude, Companionship, the Senses, the Unlucky, Repetitions, Social Awkwardness, Multiplicity

Seventy A Man in a Mirror → Solitude, Heartbreak, Houses, the Senses, the Unlucky, Blowing a Hole in the Bottom of the Boat, Reflections

Seventy-one Turnstiles → Companionship, Imbalance, Multiplicity

Seventy-two A True Story → Companionship, Heartbreak, the Senses, Never Getting Up Again, the Possible

Seventy-three Bullets and What It Takes to Dodge Them → Heartbreak, Old Age, Memory, Acceleration

Seventy-four Knees → Companionship, Houses, the Past, Memory, Repetitions, School Life

Seventy-five The Man She Is Trying to Forget → Heartbreak, Memory, Social Awkwardness, Multiplicity, the Possible

Seventy-six The Eternities → Heartbreak, Time, Repetitions, Stasis, Multiplicity

Seventy-seven Too Late → Companionship, Heartbreak, Numbers, Letters, the Unlucky, Multiplicity

Seventy-eight Detention → Companionship, Childhood, School Life

Seventy-nine I Like Your Shoes → Companionship, Numbers, Letters, Houses, Social Awkwardness

Eighty The Ghost's Disguise → Old Age, Family

Eighty-one A Source of Confusion → Childhood, Family, Balance, the Cosmos, Social Awkwardness, Multiplicity, the Apocalypse

Eighty-two Unseeable, Untouchable → Childhood, Time, Technology, Numbers, Film, the Past, Memory, Duplications, the Possible

Eighty-three Ghost Brothers → Companionship, Childhood, Balance

Eighty-four A Second True Story → Animals, Companionship, Childhood, the Lucky

Eighty-five A Life → Heartbreak, Family, the Unlucky, Blowing a Hole in the Bottom of the Boat, Social Awkwardness, Singularity

Eighty-six Extraordinary Gifts → Companionship, Family, the Unlucky, Psychic Phenomena, Social Awkwardness

Eighty-seven An Inherited Disorder → Family, Time, Imbalance, Borrowed Stories, Duplications, Social Awkwardness, Multiplicity, Singularity

Eighty-eight Prayer from an Airport Terminal → Family, the Unlucky, Social Awkwardness

Eighty-nine Hatching → Companionship, the Unlucky, Social Awkwardness, Multiplicity

Ninety Bilateral Symmetry → Space, Balance, Reflections, Multiplicity

Ninety-one Parakeets → Animals, Houses, Color, Language, the Unlucky

Ninety-two Euphemisms → Language, Memory, Forgetfulness, Social Awkwardness, Singularity

Ninety-three Roughly Eighty Grams → Solitude, Companionship, Heartbreak, Imbalance, Language, the Unlucky

✦

A NOTE ON BORROWED STORIES Several of the stories in this collection transform, echo, haunt, or needle at various preexisting materials, either conspicuously or obliquely. "The Hitchhiker," for instance, references the *Twilight Zone* episode of the same title; "Footprints," the spiritual poem known as either "Footprints" or "Footprints in the Sand." "New Life, New Civilizations" borrows its central philosophical dilemma from *Star Trek*. "The Office of Hereafters and Dissolutions," "A Moment, However Small," and "The Census" pattern themselves after stories in Giorgio Manganelli's *Centuria*. "The Runner-Up" owes a debt to the movie *Amadeus,* and "Elephants" to an anecdote contained in *Beyond Words: What Animals Think and Feel* by Carl Safina. Finally, "An Inherited Disorder" shares a set of obsessions with Adam Ehrlich Sachs's similarly titled *Inherited Disorders.*

Acknowledgments

I owe thanks to my editor, Edward Kastenmeier, and his colleague Caitlin Landuyt, who, among many other acts of assistance, helped me devise and satisfy this book's system of organization; to my agent, Jennifer Carlson, and her associates at Dunow, Carlson & Lerner, particularly Arielle Datz; to the book's art director, Kelly Blair, for bringing great sympathy and imagination to both the cover design and the interior illustrations; to my copyeditor, Lisa Silverman, and my publicist, Abigail Endler; to production editor Victoria Pearson and proofreader Amy Brosey-Láncošová, for their meticulous work; to Kyle Minor, for surprising me with an author photo that actually looks like I do to myself; to the editors of the magazines and anthologies where several of these stories were originally published, especially Deborah Treisman at *The New Yorker*, Eliza Borné at the *Oxford American*, Stanislav Rivkin at *Porter House Review*, Ben Samuel at *Bomb*, Doug Carlson at *The Georgia Review*, and Lincoln Michel and Nadxieli Nieto, the co-editors of *Tiny Nightmares: Very Short Tales of Horror*; to Brad Mooy and everyone else associated with the Arkansas Literary Festival, where roughly a quarter of the stories in this book were first tested out before an audience, and to Sam Chang and the Iowa Writers' Workshop, where a dozen of the others were; to Kathleen McHugh, for her help with the earliest manifestations of these stories; to Karen Russell, Brad Minnick, and Amy Frankel, for lending their eyes, their enthusiasm, and their sensibilities to the collection; and most especially to Amy Parker, for her encouragement, inspiration, and creative attention, and for awakening many of the ghosts in these pages.

ABOUT THE AUTHOR

In addition to *The Ghost Variations*, Kevin Brockmeier is the author of a memoir, *A Few Seconds of Radiant Filmstrip;* the novels *The Illumination*, *The Brief History of the Dead*, and *The Truth About Celia;* the story collections *Things That Fall from the Sky* and *The View from the Seventh Layer;* and the children's novels *City of Names* and *Grooves: A Kind of Mystery*. His work has been translated into seventeen languages. He has published his stories in such venues as *The New Yorker*, *The Georgia Review*, *McSweeney's*, *Zoetrope*, *Tin House*, the *Oxford American*, *The Best American Short Stories*, *The Year's Best Fantasy and Horror*, and *New Stories from the South*. He has received the Borders Original Voices Award, three O. Henry Awards (one a first prize), the PEN USA Award, a Guggenheim Fellowship, and an NEA Grant. In 2007, he was named one of *Granta* magazine's Best Young American Novelists. He teaches frequently at the Iowa Writers' Workshop, and he lives in Little Rock, Arkansas, where he was raised.

A NOTE ON THE TYPE

This book was set in Monotype Dante, a typeface designed by Giovanni Mardersteig (1892–1977). Conceived as a private type for the Officina Bodoni in Verona, Italy, Dante was originally cut for hand composition by Charles Malin, the famous Parisian punch cutter, between 1946 and 1952. Its first use was in an edition of Boccaccio's *Trattatello in laude di Dante* that appeared in 1954. The Monotype Corporation's version of Dante followed in 1957. Although modeled on the Aldine type used for Pietro Cardinal Bembo's treatise *De Aetna* in 1495, Dante is a thoroughly modern interpretation of the venerable face.

Composed by North Market Street Graphics, Lancaster, Pennsylvania
Printed and bound by Berryville Graphics, Berryville, Virginia